UNWILLINGLY TO VEGAS

Nancy Livingston was born in Stockton-on-Tees. She has worked as an actress, an air stewardess and a TV production assistant. Her radio plays have been broadcast in Great Britain and abroad, and she has written four sagas: *The Far Side of the Hill*, *The Land of Our Dreams*, *Never Were Such Times*, and *Two Sisters*. Gollancz has published all eight of Nancy Livingston's crime novels: *Trouble at Aquitaine* (winner of the Crime Writers' Association Poisoned Chalice Award), *Fatality at Bath & Wells*, *Incident at Parga*, *Death in a Distant Land* (winner of the first *Punch* prize for the best comic crime novel), *Death in Close-up*, *Mayhem in Parva*, *Unwillingly to Vegas*, and *Quiet Murder*. Nancy Livingston is married to TV director/producer David Foster and they live near Ipswich.

GW00340893

UNWILLINGLY TO VEGAS

by

Nancy Livingston

GOLLANCZ CRIME

First published in Great Britain 1991
by Victor Gollancz Ltd

First VG Crime edition published 1994
by Victor Gollancz
A Cassell imprint
Villiers House, 41/47 Strand, London WC2N 5JE

© Nancy Livingston 1991

The right of Nancy Livingston to be identified as
author of this work has been asserted by her in
accordance with the Copyright, Designs and Patents
Act, 1988.

A catalogue record for this book is
available from the British Library

ISBN 0 575 05709 2

Printed and bound in Great Britain
by Cox & Wyman Ltd, Reading

*This book is for Norm Johnson
and Frank Sinatra*

Chapter One

Sunday 11th

Louis's share of the heist would be $5,750,000. The trouble was, the job was too big and he daren't admit it, not even to himself.

The Family wasn't in the same league as the Organisation but it operated by the same rules. You joined for life, you obeyed without question; you never, never opened your mouth.

There were two branches, in New York and the West Coast. They ran the same kind of operation, usually small scale. This time they were joining forces because it was big.

It made Louis feel good to belong. He was a cuddly man. Without the protection of the Family he felt vulnerable. What if they did treat him as a gofer? He didn't mind; he was an easygoing guy.

He adored the annual reunions. Men only, so you could tell your best jokes. The venue was always a closely guarded secret, you had to know the code. Louis repeated it aloud to help him remember. Each year, when the phone call came, he'd write the message down. You weren't supposed to do that either but he was terrified he'd forget. He'd take the paper to the office and sit there till he'd worked it out. After that he'd phone Gino to check he'd got it right. If he had . . . Hell! Louis Carlson felt like James Bond!

The Family never, never tangled with the big boys or mixed with the drug scene, which made this current project all the more amazing. This time, it was really big!

Ozal was one of the bosses, officially based in New York, but he'd operated out West before. Louis had worked for him; small tasks, nothing heavy. He'd never had to give up his regular work as an associate to the associate producer of a film company, for instance. That's how he described his occupation to his mother-in-law; in reality it was even more humble. Louis was a hustler, a fixer, a gofer in films, as well. If anything wanted doing he'd volunteer; sometimes he even got used. Beth had a job, of course, otherwise they couldn't have paid the rent.

Working for Ozal was different because Louis was frightened. This time, everything had turned real sour. Louis Carlson was running as scared as a man could be without dropping dead from heart failure. He hated the feeling. He loved being happy but for the past few weeks he'd been trying to keep his head above water in a sea full of sharks.

Beth had wheedled the truth out of him, which added up to betrayal. There was only one penalty for that; Louis's palms went moist. They stayed damp when he considered the alternative: if he were to survive, he would have to double-cross the other three – Gino, his lifelong friend, Gino's nephew, John, and, most terrifying of all, Ozal.

When Ozal first called, Louis obeyed immediately. Beth still didn't understand the importance of that. She'd yelled at him once before when she'd discovered he'd given up three days' work on a Spielberg production simply because the Family needed him. On that occasion Louis had ignored her protests.

She had returned to their apartment after a couple of weeks because she couldn't stand living with her mother. She and Louis had come to an understanding after that: whenever he had private business, she wouldn't ask about it because it wasn't a subject for discussion.

This time though, Beth had asked.

Ozal had told Louis to be at a certain ice-cream stand in the park. They'd walked and Ozal had revealed his plan. Louis, stunned, scared, flattered, had reacted as he was supposed to: he'd agreed to take part. He'd told Ozal how proud he was to be included, then he'd returned to his office off West Broadway and cancelled the rental. For a week or two the phone would continue to ring but he'd be forgotten in a month. In the film business there was no such thing as an unfilled vacancy. He left no forwarding address because Ozal had ordered him to drop out of sight. By the time Beth got suspicious, it was already too late.

Today, with only seven days to go, Louis muttered a mantra to stave off increasing panic: "five comma seven five zero comma zero zero zero dollars." Less expenses, of course, but these were

8

peanuts as far as he was concerned: film contracts for unknown British actors – half of which would never be paid – plus their fifth-rate travel, plus a dummy to act as road manager. Compared to what Gino, John and Ozal had laid out, it was nothing.

Gino needed men with technical know-how like himself. Ozal had insisted these men be paid out of Gino's share: the twenty-three million would be split equally, each of them being responsible for their own team. John, for instance, had to hire the helicopter as well as bribe a coupla cops. The only major finance Louis had was in organising film trucks and a make-up wardrobe caravan, booking a few hotels; nothing to complain about.

The taxi jolting in and out of the potholes on West 46th finally came to a standstill.

"This it?"

It was raining, heavy New York rain which, if it missed you the first time, bounced back up and got you in the face. Louis peered through the blur. They were in front of an office block doorway squeezed between a scenery dock entrance and a coffee parlour.

The theatre was dark. One bad notice had killed the show. The crew, who'd set the stage only a couple of weeks previously, were hauling furniture back on to the sidewalk for reloading.

"Looks like it," Louis agreed.

"Seventeen seventy-five."

He cursed as he dodged eighteenth-century chairs and sodden plastic trees. The door to the office block swung open to the touch. The whole building was derelict. Inside it smelt of decay and the elevator wasn't working. This area was scheduled for redevelopment, the sooner the better.

Six floors up, according to Ozal. Louis began the climb. His permanent after-shave shadow was darker than ever today, his lightweight suit crumpled after the flight from London. Tension prevented him sleeping . . . only one more week. He knew how the guys on death row must feel.

His footsteps echoed through the dingy emptiness. Today was the eleventh. Seven times twenty-four – 168 hours – it wasn't just the damp which made him shiver.

Midway along the corridor he spotted the one door which was shut. The perfect place. God alone knew how Ozal had found it:

the most private place imaginable in the whole of New York City.

Once he'd gone through that door, it was the final step. Last night, in that lonely hotel room in England, listening to Beth threaten to prevent him ever seeing the kids, Louis had faced the inevitable: he had to double-cross the other three because he was in too deep to pull out.

On the flight he'd pretended there was still a choice. He could go along with Ozal or he could do it his way. Now, faced with that door, he acknowledged the truth. He was about to take on the entire Family – all by himself!

Before his heart stopped beating altogether, Louis grabbed the handle. "Plane was on time but would you believe it, I had to wait for a cab," he aimed to appear apologetic but overexcited as he crashed into the room. The others were already there. "Sorry, folks. Too much rain, I guess."

"Sure. C'm on in, Louis. Have a coffee." Ozal was expansive. "Give the man a coffee, Gino." A couple of minutes wasn't critical this morning.

Gino Millar greeted him affectionately. Medium height, swarthy, sleek dark hair, no one could mistake his Sicilian inheritance. Watching them was the unknown quantity, Gino's nephew John. He was cool. "Hi, how are you?" Louis kept his smile pinned on tight.

The plan required a helicopter pilot and Ozal needed eyes. All the same, Louis wished it could have been someone else.

He raised a scalding plastic cup to Gino, "Ciao. How's Myra?"

"Fine," he replied, "and Beth?"

"Asking after you, as usual." Warmth melted the knots in his stomach but fear made breathing difficult: whatever happened, Louis Carlson, big, amiable, stupidly fond of his wife and kids, had crossed the Rubicon.

"Let's get started." Conversation ceased. Eyes were on Ozal. "You've seen the latest on TV – the target is still twenty-three million. Everyone seems to think they'll make it, maybe more." Louis found himself squeezing the empty cup as Ozal said softly, "Let's hope they're not disappointed. OK, John, let's have the schedule."

The dates circled in red had pin-prick dots to give Ozal the same information.

"We go through it in detail, right?" he said. "You each know what your own bunch of guys has to do and let me emphasise – you are responsible. No excuses." Louis's heartbeat was painful.

"Today we tie the whole thing together. Memorise. Stop me if there's anything you don't understand."

Thousands of miles away in a London kitchen, two people were having supper. The woman was disgruntled.

"Mrs Ellis came in the pub today. She's off to visit her daughter-in-law in Los Angeles."

"Really."

Mrs Bignell sighed enviously. "Her son intends taking her everywhere. Disneyland, Malibu, Beverly Hills where the film stars live."

"Most enjoyable." Mr Pringle wasn't interested.

"D'you know what I've always dreamed about? – Coming face to face with Frank Sinatra."

"He's dead isn't he?"

Mavis Bignell looked at him pityingly. "You're thinking of Bing Crosby."

"Is that baked potato going begging?"

"Frank Sinatra is doing that charity appeal next week. Live from Las Vegas to every country in the world, like Bob Geldof. Mrs Ellis says she'll definitely be there to see it – she's going to be on the front row – she said to look out for her on the screen." No response. "You know, Las Vegas is the one place I've always wanted to see."

"I haven't." She'd roused him at last. Mr Pringle gave an uncharacteristic scowl. "Sodom and Gomorrah from what I've heard."

"Yes, but no one who visited those places ended up *disappointed* did they? Not like Benidorm."

The briefing was over. Questions had been answered; they'd been through the plan for the final time. Fear made Louis garrulous. He fingered his month-old passport. "Enrico Dulce, film producer . . . It's a great name. I've been using it for two whole weeks but I'm still not used to it."

They all had new identities. Gino was Jay Kuminsky and John, Del Freeman.

"As of now, Louis Carlson isn't in the frame," Ozal growled, "not until the eighteenth. That's when you destroy everything to do with Enrico Dulce."

"Sure, sure. I understand."

"This is my number." Each man glanced at the slip before passing it to John to add to the pile of paper already smouldering on the floor.

"You want me, you use that number from now on, OK? Not my home. But as from midnight on the seventeenth, I cannot be contacted there either," Ozal emphasised.

None of them would meet after the seventeenth, it was part of the deal. Louis would miss Gino and Myra. He wondered sentimentally if they felt the same about him. Which brought him back, reluctantly, to Beth.

The trouble was his wife was too bright. Ozal had warned him. Louis had tried to think of a tale to deflect her from asking awkward questions; it was impossible. Eventually, in off-hand fashion, he told her they were about to leave home for a long, long vacation. Beth reacted slowly at first.

"You sure?"

"Sure, I'm sure."

"I mean, how can we afford it?"

Louis had sniggered, that had been his first mistake. "Don't worry about that, honey," was his second. Their joint account was almost empty.

Beth stared a long time before saying in an odd tone, "Will I have to see to the dogs?"

"What?"

"Is it the kind of 'vacation' where we don't come back – ever?" Silence. "OK, in plain language, Louis, do I have to take them to be killed or will you do it?"

"For Chrissakes – "

"Come on, lover. If you mean what I think you mean, one of us has to be a murderer. All I'm asking is: who will the kids blame afterwards?"

"Maybe you could find someone who wants a coupla dogs . . . " It was feeble.

"Louis, you have been lying awake for weeks. It's something so big you're terrified, so it has to be spectacular. If you're involved, why draw attention to yourself by hawking our two pooches around the neighbourhood? You tell me we're leaving here for good. What I'm asking is how long have I got?" He tried to stall but she practically spat out the words.

"How long, Louis?"

"About a fortnight, I guess."

Beth leaned forward so that he couldn't avoid her gaze. "When, exactly?"

"The seventeenth." After that, he knew she would work out the rest for herself.

Later, in the big double bed with its fancy drapes, resentment came in waves: she'd be leaving everything behind. Louis wanted to tell her she could have the moon – after the seventeenth. He didn't dare, he'd said too much already.

Ozal's voice, silky soft, seemed to penetrate his thoughts. "What have you told Beth?" Louis's throat was dry. To his relief Ozal then asked Gino, "What about Myra?"

"She knows enough," Gino replied. "I kinda warned her we could be on the move real soon."

"That's what I told Beth," Louis said eagerly. "She asked a few questions but not much. I guess she's accepted it."

Which was blatantly untrue. After that restless night, she'd suddenly accused him.

"It's Ozal, isn't it? He's behind this one." In the silence, she'd whispered, "Goddamn you for being so stupid!"

Now out of fear, Louis overdid his enthusiasm.

"Enrico Dulce, it's a helluva name for a film producer!"

They all knew the penalty for betrayal.

John Millar watched covertly. It was his duty to report what he saw. Not that Ozal missed much. Once John had found his own hand being seized. Ozal had murmured, "Don't try it, kid. Whatever you're thinking, don't try and convince yourself you're smarter than I am."

They'd never referred to it again. Gradually John's confidence returned, especially today, when ordered to observe the other two.

Louis Carlson was a strange choice. Why was the man so nervous? OK, his knowledge of the film business was part of the plan. When they'd discussed what he had to do, Louis had come up with various suggestions. Now he was sweating like a pig and a frightened man could be a liability.

Neither Louis nor Gino had been told the whole of it, Ozal had kept certain details back. John knew and was elated: it would give him the necessary edge – afterwards. For it was John's secret intention to double-cross. Two shares, maybe three, would give him leverage. He was aiming high: nothing less than to become head of the Family, as soon as possible.

Louis would have to be disposed of, also Beth Carlson. That was surely what Ozal intended? He'd muttered to John that Beth was too intelligent and John understood. He would take care of them after the heist. He would go along with Ozal as long as was necessary – but what about his uncle?

Dare he suggest to Ozal that Gino was untrustworthy? The realisation that a man's life could hinge on his word gave John a bigger kick than sex.

Gino was uneasy. How old was his nephew? Twenty-six or seven? Myra would know. He'd been recruited last year after leaving the army – precipitately. Gino never had learned the full history of that but rumours began as soon as John joined the Family. He'd acquitted himself almost too well, he'd been so ruthless. What worried Gino much more was that John now appeared indispensible to Ozal.

He gave himself a mental shake. Ozal needed eyes. John was the obvious choice. Who else could have undertaken his special role with the police in California? That hadn't been easy to fix.

But there was another, even more serious, worry as far as Gino was concerned: Beth Carlson.

His wife, Myra, was one of the Family. Ozal trusted her. He'd been adamant about Beth though. "Don't tell her a thing, Louis, however much you're tempted."

"I won't, I swear."

"Beth's – unpredictable. Suppose . . . " Ozal made it sound like a joke, which it wasn't. "Suppose she saw it as her duty to tell somebody?" That time, Louis had looked sick. Today, he had verbal diarrhoea.

"There's no point in calling *my* number either," he babbled to Ozal. "As of yesterday my family have left home. Beth has taken both the boys. You want I should tell *you* where, Ozal?"

"No!"

Gino shifted uncomfortably. Why the hell couldn't Louis keep quiet? All the same, why had Beth disappeared so soon? He waited but Louis didn't explain. Instead Ozal thumped the table, "Louis, no one tells anybody. It's goodbye, OK?" He tried to sound bluff, "Hey, I don't even want to know which part of the *world* you guys will be in."

"It's the only way," Gino offered sympathetically.

John said what was on everyone's mind, "If anyone talks, the rest could end up dead, so he has to go." The room felt cold after that.

John would have to go anyway, thought Ozal. Arrogant, ambitious, far too ready to act on his own. He had his uses, of course. He could take care of Louis and Beth before he was disposed of. Maybe it could be fixed to look like a double killing gone wrong? Ozal liked the sound of that, he'd think about it some more. Maybe Gino could arrange it.

He frowned. How would Gino react? Myra was OK. Gino's part in the plan was based on his electronic wizardry but the guy could be a pain in the butt. Ozal sighed and thrust the worry to the back of his mind.

"What time are you casting tomorrow, Louis?"

"Eleven. The agency has arranged the auditions. No one famous, like you said. A coupla has-beens who need a break from commercials, a kid from drama school, etc. Not many of them have been in the US of A before."

Ozal nodded. "That's important."

"Hell, this will be a great production," Louis joked. "It might never get finished but what there is of it will make Oscar material!" Ozal didn't bother to smile.

"The road manager has to be *reliable* but dumb."

"I put out a coupla feelers. I've got a name."

As dumb as Louis in fact. Ozal gave an inward smile.

"John, the helicopter is booked out as from tomorrow?"

"Yes."

"Let's see the map reference, Gino. The place sounds just about perfect."

Gino tried to conjure up the picture. "It's a barn, about a mile from the highway and away from the ranch, hidden by some tall rocks. The ranch is owned by a woman and her grandson – he's a dumbo."

"You'd be surprised at the number of my regulars who've been to

Florida instead of Spain this year," Mavis Bignell said wistfully. "It's not that much more expensive apparently."

"I wonder they noticed the difference." Mr Pringle warmed to his theme. "By all accounts, Spanish is the lingua franca over there and Florida has one of the highest murder rates per capita in the whole of the United States – "

"Oh, give over!" Mavis thumped the pillow on her side of the bed. "Proper killjoy you can be, sometimes."

They watched as John swept the ashes into a plastic sack. No trace of their visit remained.

"Saying goodbye's the hardest part, eh, Gino?" Louis was obviously close to tears.

"Best not count our chickens," Gino murmured, "it's bad luck."

What had luck got to do with it? thought John contemptuously, that sort of talk was weak.

"Guess that's it, Ozal."

"You 100 per cent sure?"

John scrutinised the room. "It's clean."

"OK, let's go. Louis first."

Louis hugged Ozal impulsively. "So long old friend."

"Take care." Ozal sounded sincere.

"Will do." Louis clasped Gino then John. "Good luck . . . Same to you, kid. May the good Lord bless our enterprise." He'd embarrassed them.

After a pause, Gino said, "Amen."

The echoing footsteps faded. For the first time Gino acknowledged to himself what the outcome might be for Louis: there would be no appeal. If Louis blundered, sentence would be carried out immediately.

He mustn't think about it. He touched Ozal briefly on the shoulder. "Bye, John," he called and went quickly downstairs. On the sidewalk, the scene hands were still loading furniture but there was no sign of Louis. Gino ducked his dark head against the rain and began to walk.

On his way back to JFK, Louis wiped away the sweat. It was worse than he'd figured. Thank God fate had already shown him a way out. In that slum of a London theatrical agency, a face from the past had stared up at him from the pages of *Spotlight*. He hadn't yet worked out how she could help him but there must be a way.

His life was safe until midnight on the seventeenth because his role was crucial. After that it was reasonable to suppose he would be their first target. He'd seen it today in John's eyes; gun or a knife, that gaze had said, or maybe even with his bare hands like the army had taught him. Although she didn't realise it, Beth was probably scheduled as the encore.

She'd sworn unless he broke free, she'd go for a divorce. She'd apply for custody of the boys. Louis knew she meant it but dead women don't carry out threats. He didn't want her dead, he loved her! They were safe enough for the present, although Ozal was bound to guess she and the kids were with her mother in Boston.

He prayed Gino would understand about the double-cross, that mattered a lot. Gino might not care what happened to John – but Ozal? Maybe Gino would go along with that, too. No point in worrying about it until he'd worked out what he was going to do.

There'd be no executions, that wasn't Louis's way. He had a gun for threatening people but he hadn't fired it in years. Back in that dingy, crummy office this morning, Louis had felt like Judas. The enormity of what he was about to do made him sweat even more.

The following morning in the theatrical agency in the Charing Cross Road, the receptionist was adamant. "A valid passport was what I said. You can't audition unless you've got one."

"Avril, if I get the part, I swear I'll fill in the form immediately – "

She was shaking her head. "There isn't time! Today's Monday. Everyone has to be prepared to fly out to the States on Wednesday."

"You're joking!"

"That's why Mr Dulce has to cast all four parts this morning. A New York agency recommended us to him. He made contact last week, selected you from our books, phoned yesterday to confirm he was on his way and landed at Gatwick an hour ago." Avril fanned herself with a script. "I've never known a week like it – but no one's reading for him unless I've checked the expiry date in their passport." One was proffered and she glanced through it rapidly.

"Thanks Monica, that's fine."

"Don't we need work permits? What about American Equity?"

"Mr Dulce's dealt with all that. You'll get normal tourist visas on the aircraft and that's all you have to complete."

"And we leave on Wednesday? It's incredible!"

Avril nodded. "But worth it. A four-week shoot with locations in Colorado, California and Nevada. He only got confirmation from his backers over the weekend, he said. Now he can offer 15 per cent above your normal fees because of the rush, plus expenses. So, can I assume everyone here is interested?"

Through an enthusiastic chorus, Monica Moffat asked, "Do we know any details? Where the actual locations are, for instance?"

Avril scanned the front of the script. "I read this in bed last night. There are four smashing parts. Some of the places are mentioned . . . Las Vegas." Whistles from the group. "Here, take a look." As others clustered round the script, she motioned the actress aside, "Mr Dulce particularly asked for you Monica, after he'd seen your commercials tape."

"Very flattering!" Monica Moffat gave a brief laugh. "Why not? I'm game to read for him anyway."

"Thanks." Avril ticked her name as another, less well-known actress, pushed forward.

"Darling, my passport's up to date and I'd be willing to go to *Mars* on Wednesday. What's the catch?"

"None. Casting today, wardrobe appointments tomorrow, depart on Wednesday."

"When do we study? During the flight?"

"Sounds like it."

"But how can we get the *feel* of our parts?" asked a young blonde unknown.

"Forget the method, ducky, just don't bump into the furniture. What's the production company's track record, Avril?"

"No one's heard of them but he's paying cash up front – "

"Wonderful!" Most of the group had been out of work for months and were disinclined to quibble.

"What's he like?"

"Mr Dulce? Big, very American. Dark eyes . . . sexy!"

"*Rainbow Journey*" a character lady read aloud. "It's a sweet title."

"Especially if it includes a pot of gold!"

Mr Pringle had a suspicion that this burly, sweaty American was trying to steam-roller him. "What I can't understand is how you came to hear of me, Mr Dulce? I've seldom worked in – show business – except in a very small capacity."

"Your name was suggested to me last week by a very fine British television producer," Louis insisted. "Jonathan P Powell?"

Mr Pringle was poker-faced.

"You remember, dear," Mrs Bignell said impatiently, "you helped out when his mother was strangled."

"I happened to be in the vicinity, Mavis, in no way was I connected – "

"Mr Dulce met Jonty in Soho last week and when Jonty heard they needed an accountant for this film, he thought of you straightaway."

"Mavis, I am not an accountant, I am a retired civil servant, having spent my working life in the Inland Revenue."

The heavily jowled American spoke as though he hadn't heard, "Jonathan was advising me on the casting and when I explained the problem, he came up with your name, sir. You see, this production needs an honest man."

Only one, Louis thought, but they had to be sure of him.

Mr Pringle was too worried to respond: surely even in America there was an accountant of sufficient probity?

"I assist people with tax returns and VAT problems in order to boost my pension," he explained to Louis. "I also audit the accounts of the West Merton Fur and Feather Club, in an honorary capacity you understand, nothing *arduous*."

Behind the bar, Mavis Bignell saw the incredible prospect of a free trip to America, all expenses paid – with the distinct possibility of a visit to Las Vegas – begin to fade.

"Don't be hasty, dear. You never know, you might be clever enough." She smiled at the American. "What exactly would Mr Pringle have to do, Mr Dulce?"

Louis Carlson described supervising the payroll of a small film unit and dealing with expenses.

"You'd take care of the day to day running costs, hotels and suchlike. Shooting is scheduled to last approximately four weeks. Transportation is being arranged by my office in New York, also accommodation and expenses. You would be responsible for settling facility fees and keeping the budget generally on target. Your fee would be five thousand dollars, one thousand up-front."

"How much is that in real money?" asked Mavis, conversationally.

Mr Pringle frowned. "Four weeks is a long time." It would mean having to arrange for that wretched boy next door to mow the lawn.

"It could be less," Louis assured him. "Your air ticket would be left open."

"I don't really think . . . "

But the American hadn't time to waste. "Mrs Bignell is included, naturally," he said turning on his full charm just as Mavis finished her mental arithmetic.

"Here . . . you'll get over two and a half thousand pounds!"

"Plus a screen credit."

"A what?" asked Mr Pringle.

"At the end of the picture, when the names roll through?"

"Yes?"

"Yours will be up there, among the stars." Mr Dulce spread his hands to indicate the size of the lettering. "Company accountant, G D H Pringle."

"Oh, no." Mr Pringle was emphatic, "My qualifications do not merit such an exaggeration – "

"OK, OK, we'll come up with an alternative."

"As a matter of interest," asked Mavis, "who are the stars in your picture?" The American drained his glass.

"You mix a mean daiquiri, ma'am. Same again all round, including yourself. Did I mention," he added casually, "that the travel arrangements include riding the dog? Anyone visiting the States the first time should definitely experience that, it's part of our culture."

Mr Pringle was surprised. He hadn't realised huskies were in common use outside the Arctic Circle.

★

Later, Louis phoned Ozal.

"I've found the roadie all right. He thinks that five thousand is too much – "

"What!"

"We have to include his lady friend – she won't be any trouble. All *she* wants is to meet Frank Sinatra." There was laughter across the Atlantic.

"How dumb can you get!"

"The man's reliable, I've checked him out."

"Perfect," murmured Ozal.

Louis took his courage in both hands. "I'd like to use an old friend of yours in my picture, Ozal . . . she'd be perfect for the main part."

"Which . . . old friend?"

Louis mentioned a name.

"No!"

"Please," Louis begged. "She could do with the work and she's a great little actress. The two of you will never meet, so where's the harm?"

When Ozal replied, he was icy.

"God help you if we do, Louis."

Mavis, naturally optimistic, dwelt on the advantages.

"We'll see America and it won't cost us a bean! You hadn't got any particular plans for the next few weeks?"

"I had planned to visit the exhibition at the Tate and my library books are overdue," he said with dignity. "Besides, why ask me? There must be thousands of better qualified men over there."

"Didn't Mr Dulce say this was an all-British production, to avoid American labour laws?"

That part of the explanation had been so vague it bothered Mr Pringle even more.

"I must confess I didn't fully understand – "

"Talk about looking a gift horse; maybe Jonty Powell wanted to do you a good turn? Not everyone gets offered a trip like this, all expenses paid. Yes, dear, what'll it be?" She broke off to serve a group in the bar.

"Tell you what, let's sleep on it. If you feel the same in the morning, we'll call the whole thing off," she said, to mollify him.

★

The following morning those who'd been cast were back at the agency to sign their contracts. Already the prospect of work had had its bracing effect. Ivor Henry was euphoric.

"I can't wait, my darlings. Is this your first visit to the States, Monica?"

"I was in New York briefly, years ago."

"I didn't know," said the receptionist, surprised.

"It was in the sixties. Off Broadway. The play was pretty dire but in those days that wasn't so important. What was wonderful was *sailing* across the Atlantic."

"Five glorious days in which to relax, eh?" said Ivor. "Who's playing the young dare-devil, Avril?"

"Jed Pointer," she answered cautiously.

"Oh, my God!"

"Mr Dulce insisted he looked right for the part."

"So he does," Ivor Henry said bitterly, "as it calls for a drunken tearaway who smashes hotel rooms to pieces. All in a day's work for Jed. I thought Dulce wanted *actors*, not louts."

"What time is my wardrobe appointment?" Monica Moffat interrupted tactfully.

"Eleven."

"Just time for a coffee."

"I'll join you, if I may. Anything to delay the inevitable meeting with Jed."

"Don't forget your tickets," said Avril. "First stop, Denver."

"Denver? I assumed we'd be going direct to LA?"

Avril shrugged. "It must be nearer the first location. It's a charter flight."

"In a pukka aer-o-plane, I trust," Ivor demanded, "with a wing on either side? One can't be too careful these days. Some of us have a live-in lover to support."

She giggled. "You'll be all right. The company have even employed an accountant to look after you."

"We live in changing times." He settled his balding cashmere stylishly. "In the old days one had a dresser and a personal make-up artiste, useful people like that. Now all we get is a money man. I trust he's tough enough to deal with friend Jed."

"Bound to be," Avril soothed.

"Such a comfort." He kissed her on both cheeks. "Au revoir, precious. What shall I bring you as a souvenir?"

"Fifth Avenue. All of it."

"Greedy!"

That evening, in her tiny shabby flat in Notting Hill, Monica Moffat gazed unseeing at the dusty greenery outside and argued with her conscience. It had been a long time ago. She'd vowed never to return but passion had faded; time had healed a raw, almost broken, heart and after all these years she couldn't possibly bump into him. In other words there was absolutely no reason not to accept the contract.

It was a good part; she needed one badly. Her career was in the doldrums, she was short of money. That was an understatement, she was broke. Then there was Dulce himself, a persuasive man. They'd gossiped about theatre; he seemed sympathetic. She thought she would enjoy working with him.

Monica glanced at the expensive, glamorous garments the wardrobe buyer had chosen this morning. "Wish I was coming with you," the girl had said, "but according to Mr Dulce, the crew have to be American because of the labour laws."

"I'm sorry, too."

"Good luck."

The risk of an encounter was a chance in a million; a chance Monica was prepared to take.

Chapter Two

Monday 12th

The old barn was some distance from the farm, under the lee of a rocky outcrop. The track to it was overgrown. Newer, prefabricated storage had been erected nearer the homestead, although this housed little nowadays beyond what was necessary to tend a few head of cattle.

When Shirley and Cal first came, they'd had energy. From the verandah they'd gazed across dusty land at traffic on the highway.

"Trucks will travel that route with our produce one day," Cal had promised, "that's why this is such an ideal spot."

It felt like the end of the line now to the former GI bride.

Shirley had grown up in an overcrowded Lancashire terrace. Here in Nevada, her nearest neighbour was five miles distant. The only contact with other living souls was those anonymous truck drivers. She would sit for hours on the verandah watching the toy-sized vehicles, dreaming how they must live their lives.

Cal had had his dreams, he'd swept her off her feet. She'd been a factory girl. They met jiving on the dance floor at the King's Hall, Belle Vue. The girl from Salford had listened to descriptions of a ranch. She knew what cowboys were from films but she couldn't remember where Nevada was. Cal licked a finger and drew a map on the glass table top.

"It's a state out west, honey . . . but I ain't no cowhand. The ranch isn't much of a property, neither," he'd warned. "It's real neglected. But it could be something. We could make it nice. All it needs is work."

He'd given it all he'd got but the land was unrelenting. After Cal's death it had taken only months for dust to silt up the furrows and for tumbleweed to bowl in and take hold. All that remained to mark her husband's passage upon earth, as well as that of their son Keith and his wife, were the wire fences and prefabricated buildings, and the small grave plot.

Inside, fancy curtains put up by Keith's wife had faded because of the sun. Outside, with no one to tend the crop, vulnerable shoots had shrivelled before they could grow. Cal had watched helplessly as the cancer which began after the fatal car crash took an ever fiercer hold. He'd endured nine months of it; every fresh attempt to keep him alive consumed another slice of their savings. Finally, there was nothing left. Shirley sat by his bedside, watching apathetically as decay encroached from every side.

At sixty-eight she was a widow without hope. There was no money for pretty clothes or the beauty shop. Worse, there was insufficient to pay the bills. Come the fall it was inevitable the bank would foreclose.

If only her grandson had inherited Cal's vision or Keith's strength. Instead, Sammy was simple minded. He'd been flung clear when the car skidded under the truck. Shirley often wondered if there'd been a blow to his skull but the doctors, mindful of insurance claims, were non-committal. And now Sammy had been lured into some crazy scheme by a stranger.

It would soon be dark. On the highway headlights gleamed and the sound Shirley had been dreading all day approached over the low rocky hills.

"Looks like they're here," she called. The fly-screen creaked; Sammy shielded his eyes against the dying sun.

"Told you they'd come!" he cried exultantly. "You didn't believe me, did you, Grandma? You going to do what I asked? They said it was a secret."

"So you keep saying." She rose, brushing insects from her skirt.

"Tell me one more time so's I know you understand," he demanded. It was the phrase she used when instructing him what to do. The helicopter was much closer now.

"I'm to stay out of sight. Forget I ever saw them, whoever they are. Oh, Sammy, I do wish you hadn't got yourself mixed up – " but he'd pressed a hand over her mouth.

"Ssh, Grandma, I know what I'm doing. This way we can pay off the bank." His eyes were blue, like Keith's, but vacuous. He had a childlike eagerness to please. Shirley cursed herself for even mentioning their debts.

"Listen, love, there's got to be some other way. We don't know anything about these people."

"He's a nice man, Grandma. Real polite. All he wants is to see our old barn."

Then why all the secrecy, she wanted to shout; if he's honest, why creep down over the hills in a helicopter?

Sammy leaped down the steps and into the pick-up. It made her angry to see he'd put on his best boots for this meeting. "Go inside now, like you promised," he begged.

A plume of dust marked his progress along the old track. He must've dipped the headlights; the helicopter blinked its own beam in reply. As it began to descend, Shirley went inside and jerked at the blinds. If the strangers didn't want to be seen, neither did she.

It was when she'd driven out in search of a bale of wire, she'd discovered the new padlock on the barn. Holes in the fabric had been patched, it was impossible to see inside. Later when she'd demanded to know why, Sammy had been sullen, telling her it was none of her business.

It wasn't in his nature to sustain a mood. He knelt beside her chair that evening. "I've made you tea, Grandma, the way you like it." Would they have recognised it in Salford? Shirley wondered wryly. No matter how often she showed him it was always a lone tea-bag floating in lukewarm water.

"Thanks, love."

It had been a casual meeting in the local bar. Shirley's apprehension increased when she heard. Local folk poked fun at her grandson; had one of them introduced him to the stranger? When she asked, Sammy pretended not to hear.

"That ol' barn's convenient for the highway, Grandma," his words were a mocking echo of Cal's. "Trucks can come in and out and be on their way with no bother. Mr Kuminsky said his company is willing to pay good money."

"But why, Sammy? What sort of goods does he want to store out there?" Fear came big and strong. "Sammy, it's not drugs?" He thrust out his lower lip.

"I ain't a fool, Grandma." But sadly, she knew that he was.

Your father wouldn't have been so daft, nor your grandad, she thought. Photos of Cal and Keith, sealed in the aspic of time, gave no comfort.

Tonight, one of the grey plaits had worked loose. Shirley pushed it back under her headscarf. Her hair used to be in tight curls in the Belle Vue days. She'd used wire pipe-cleaners every night to keep them that way. She'd worn full skirts with bunchy petticoats and an elastic belt to cinch her waist . . .

It was time to feed the calves. She reached automatically for the overall behind the door, then she remembered.

Walking through to Sammy's room at the back Shirley focused the binoculars. The helicopter was out of sight behind the barn. Whoever they were, they were being extremely discreet.

From the forbidden place beneath the quilt came a pathetic yelp; Sammy's mutt, Bomber, protesting at her neglect. Shirley groped to fondle the uneven ears.

"You're bloody stupid an' all,' she complained in her flat Lancashire voice. "You're not supposed to be here, but you can't help telling me for fear I won't give you a cuddle." The tail thumped. "He must've wanted to impress them if he didn't take you with him, eh Bomber?" Maybe Sammy was growing up at last? She sighed.

Bomber's "training" had occupied the last few weeks of Cal's life. Every evening, Shirley was forced to listen to Sammy out in the yard, imploring Bomber to leap through hoops as Cal, his mind clouded with drugs, devised ever more desperate stratagems to provide for them both.

She made an effort now to slough off despair. "Something's bound to turn up, eh Bomber?" she whispered again.

The helicopter engine started up. She returned to the kitchen and when Sammy finally reappeared, said tiredly, "Calves haven't been fed yet."

"Let me tell you first, Grandma," he pleaded. "It's honest business. They need clean dry storage, that's all. For packaging materials an' paper. Mr Kuminsky went over every square inch, checking it was OK.'

"Packaging materials?"

He laughed at her expression. "Knew you wouldn't believe me," he said triumphantly. "When I told them, they gave me a piece. Here . . . " Shirley fingered the corrugated cardboard gingerly. "It's top quality. It's only for a month or two, a coupla deliveries and a few trucks coming to collect, he said. They're willing to pay two thousand dollars. Here . . . " Sammy held out a fist full of bills. "Half in advance. I counted it and signed a receipt," he finished proudly.

"Why all the fuss?" asked Shirley. "Why not use a regular warehouse?"

"Their old place was asking too much for a new lease. They're negotiating with a depot in Santa Fé but they needed somewhere meantime."

"They?"

"Mr Freeman was piloting the helicopter. The nice one's called Mr Kuminsky."

Shirley wondered if either man was genuine.

"You're not still mad at me, Grandma?" Sam pleaded.

"No, love." She sighed. It was only for a month or so and what could be criminal about storing cardboard? Cal had said they should make use of the buildings. Maybe Sammy had been right for once. "I'll pay this money into the bank," she told him. He gave a sly wink.

"We mustn't tell anyone where it came from, remember? That's part of the deal."

"I'll remember." But if the state police did come asking questions, Mr Freeman and Mr Kuminsky could look out for themselves.

Sammy felt disappointed to see the money tucked away inside the old leather purse. If only he'd kept a few dollars back, he could've taken Charlene into town.

Grandma didn't like Charlene. She never said so but Sammy knew. Charlene preferred meeting him in town. It was expensive because she liked to gamble. Everything was expensive for Sammy, even gas for the pick-up cost money.

It had turned into a nightmare, worse than Mr Pringle's gloomiest forebodings. Early yesterday morning – or was it the day before? He'd lost his grip on time, he'd put back the hour hand on his watch so often – the phone had rung just as he and Mavis were leaving for the airport.

Enrico Dulce was fulsomely apologetic but he'd had to go on ahead, "To check a few things out". Mr Pringle would find comprehensive instructions plus cash for everyone's expenses in an envelope at the airline check-in counter. All that was necessary was to make sure the cast caught the flight. It was as he replaced the receiver that Mr Pringle realised he'd virtually been put in charge.

They'd reached New York without incident. Only slightly harassed, Mr Pringle had supervised the transfer from John F Kennedy to La Guardia and eventually discovered the right departure channel for Denver.

In answer to questions from Ivor Henry and Jed Pointer, he repeated his instructions; Enrico Dulce hoped to meet them at Denver but if not, he would leave further details at the airport.

"So we don't know where we shall be staying?" Monica Moffat didn't appear annoyed like the others and for that Mr Pringle was thankful. She was, in his opinion, much more of a lady.

"Not yet, I fear," he apologised. He had already discovered the actors knew even less than he did, which surprised him, but they were accustomed to the vagaries of filming and Mr Pringle was not. They gossiped unconcernedly as the internal flight landed, first at St Louis, before taking off on the final leg.

Mavis scolded. What was the point in worrying, she demanded. Weren't they following that nice Mr Dulce's instructions to the letter? Mr Pringle agreed that they were. Well then, he should stop fretting and enjoy the view. Down there was America.

"And that's the wide Missouri. We used to sing about that when I was at school. I bet you never imagined you'd see it."

But at Denver, his fears were fully realised. Once again, Dulce had come and gone leaving instructions at the airport counter. Mr Pringle opened the second envelope. This time the note instructed the party to proceed to a minibus outside the terminal buildings; this had been booked to take them to their next destination.

Jed and Ivor enquired eagerly among the various vehicles. When found, the driver was taciturn.

"Pringle and party? Sure, get inside." He seemed not to hear when Ivor asked the name of the hotel but no one cared. This was Denver; they had arrived.

They marvelled light-heartedly at the variety of houses with shady trees and small neat gardens, the modest skyscrapers backed by a vista of distant rocky mountains, but when the minibus finally turned in at a depot, incredulity was followed by outrage.

"Greyhound!" Ivor Henry exploded. "You cannot be serious! Did you know about this, Pringle? Why aren't we staying here? We were told we were coming to Denver so where the hell are we off to now?" Alas, Mr Pringle didn't know. He went tiredly up to reception.

"Sure we've an envelope for you, Mr Pringle, sir. And six Ameripasses." These sounded like invitations to a party but looked suspiciously like more tickets.

"Your coach is due to leave in ten minutes," the girl warned. "Service 365 from Gate 2. Leave the baggage, we'll take care of it."

Deaf to further protests, Mr Pringle shepherded his group aboard.

He had travelled in a coach once before, when Mrs Bignell had fancied a trip with the over-sixties to Weston-super-Mare. That too had been a mistake.

The rest of the passengers were a mixed bunch; over-sixties were in evidence but so too were students with hulking great backpacks blocking the aisle. Miffed, the four thespians huddled together at the rear. Mavis had, very wisely, chosen seats as far from them as possible.

Mr Pringle acknowledged her efforts to keep up their flagging spirits: during the interminable check-in queues at Gatwick, the hours aloft forced to watch Lucille Ball and finally here on the coach.

"You can't watch scenery from a plane," she insisted valiantly. "It'll be a novelty. Provided we don't take too long getting to wherever it is."

She also told him what she'd learned of their travelling companions. "Monica Moffat is the only real star. She does adverts nowadays but I once saw her in a late-night film. Ivor Henry was a Gestapo officer in 'Allo, 'allo. Jed Pointer was in the papers for being rude on a chat show." The last artiste baffled her, "I don't think I've ever seen Clarissa thing before. Perhaps she's a beginner."

Jed wasn't shy. He had demanded money in a menacing attitude before their first aircraft had reached cruising altitude. "You in charge of the float?" Mr Pringle blinked. "I'll have a hundred to be going on with."

"Provided you sign a receipt, certainly – "

"No autographs. My agent doesn't like it," Jed smirked.

"And show me some form of identification."

He was affronted. "Listen, mate, my latest series is still going out on Channel 4."

"Ah . . . " Mr Pringle was sad, "I was burgled recently. I haven't replaced the set; it didn't seem worthwhile."

"And we never watch Channel 4 in the Bricklayers," Mavis told him.

From Denver they headed south down the shining, spiralling highway that led to Colorado Springs. The Rockies went unheeded as Mr Pringle tried to decipher the latest instructions.

"This ticket . . . " Mavis was examining her Ameripass. "It says unlimited travel for seven days."

"Oh dear, oh dear!"

"I expect Mr Dulce will have arranged a rest for us soon," she sounded strained. "I hope so. My feet are swelling up."

Mr Pringle refused to allow himself to hope; instead he said quietly, "There's a hotel voucher in this envelope. As far as I can make out, we're due to stay at a place called Flagstaff. Can you find it on the map?"

Mavis examined the rest of Colorado then New Mexico. "America's a big place, isn't it? Oh, here we are – Flagstaff, Arizona."

"Arizona?" Mr Pringle looked at the scale, at the Greyhound timetable and then re-examined the voucher. "Is this for tonight or tomorrow night?" he asked. "I don't even know which day it is any longer."

Mrs Bignell's optimism sagged. "I'll tell you something else, dear. I didn't want to worry you earlier but I may have left the gas on."

"Oh, good Lord!"

She sighed, "I know. I'm sorry. D'you think it's worth phoning your next-door neighbour?"

"It was such a rush, I forgot to leave her a key."

"Ah." They sat, picturing the conflagration and wondering whether the insurance company would pay up. Eventually, Mavis said, "We'd better not tell the others we're going as far as Arizona."

"No."

"Especially Jed." Mr Pringle agreed whole-heartedly. "Let them enjoy the ride. The scenery here's quite nice. Better than Weston."

They ate Big Macs at Raton and watched with sinking hearts as a quarrel began among the coach drivers, but amid the anxiety Mr Pringle marvelled that the thespians appeared to be recovering. All except Jed, of course.

"I should've had a limo. There's always a clause in my contract says I should. To protect my image."

"I have no knowledge of your contract," Mr Pringle said firmly.

"The hotel had better be good then. When do we get there?" Mavis provided a diversion.

"Oh, look . . . Frank Sinatra!"

On the screen above the food counter, the Star was seen slipping away from his eyrie, protected by sunglasses and guards, on his way to raise millions of dollars for deprived children. Banks, they were told, were preparing to flood Las Vegas with vast amounts of money in anticipation of public generosity, for this was an appeal with a difference: the cash would be on view.

"Every dollar you donate will be seen on camera!" the hyped voice shrieked. "Every cent or dollar bill. Why not make your contribution the BIG ONE!"

"I wonder if Mrs Ellis has got there yet," Mavis said enviously. To the waitress wiping their table she explained, "She's a friend of mine from England. She was planning to be in Las Vegas for that appeal. She was hoping to get a ringside seat."

"She'd better be rich then. Those are costing near enough one thousand dollars apiece."

"Fancy! Oh well, she'll be nearer the back. She only has her pension, you see."

By Albuquerque, they'd had enough. It was dark. They stopped at a Chevron garage in a bare red landscape with yet more gaunt mountains. Mavis still tried, occasionally, to provide points of interest. "The last town, Santa Fé, was where John Wayne rode out into the sunset." Her companion grunted.

Mr Pringle had now experienced every manifestation of bad temper among the actors, apart from Monica Moffat whose silence was reproach enough. In vain he protested to Ivor Henry the schedule wasn't of his making and that Dulce alone was responsible. The four needed someone to blame and Mr Pringle was there.

Under the hot New Mexican night sky his voice cracked as he broke the last, unwelcome piece of news. Here at Albuquerque they were due to change coaches. Another endless stretch of road, covered by schedule number 577, lay between them and Flagstaff, where rooms had been reserved. Before their anger could burst forth, he hurried inside with their Ameripasses.

The booking clerk was puzzled. "Why didn't they check your group through to your destination? That's what we usually do."

"I don't know." He'd been obeying instructions and knew no better. "We hadn't much time at Denver, the coach was ready to leave."

A wonderful thought occurred. If there weren't enough seats, why not stay here? There was sufficient money in the float. What did the blessed hotel voucher matter? It was cruelty to adults to make them continue; he would telephone Dulce and tell him so.

But even as he thought of it, Mr Pringle realised he hadn't a phone number. They were being despatched half-way across a continent by a man from a secret lair.

The clerk checked her computer screen. Behind her on yet another television, Mr Pringle watched as the Star descended into Las Vegas in his own private helicopter. Despite the temperature, Mr Sinatra looked cool and casual. Mr Pringle tasted his own stale breath; even his underwear, clean on for the journey, felt as if he'd been living in it for a week.

"It's a great time to be visiting the States," the clerk said proudly. "We're going to prove to the world America's still got a lotta heart when it comes to deprived kids."

"Yes, indeed."

"This depot has collected over four hundred and eighty dollars."

"Very commendable."

"Even if we don't make the five hundred, we'll see it go down the chute." Realising he didn't understand, she explained, "The banks are delivering the pledges, then the money's going down a big chute into this enormous golden bowl. Hey look, there's the model!"

A shot of a glittering gold container appeared, surrounded by photographs of curvaceous young women wearing strategically small amounts of dollar bills.

"If we top the five hundred, everyone from the depot will see their names on that screen – the entire world will see them – can you imagine!"

Her eyes were shining now. "There'll be enough in that bowl to feed every starving kid by the time we've finished . . . " She was a tubby girl with an ugly oily skin but she was almost beautiful as she repeated, "Twenty-three million dollars!" Mr Pringle made a mental note to increase his contribution to Help the Aged.

"If it's not possible to make those six reservations to Flagstaff –" he began but she dashed his hopes.

"No, that's OK. That service is only half full tonight." She detached six counterfoils and handed back the passes. "Have a good day."

They'd gone through another time zone: it was 4.00 a.m. on Friday. Mr Pringle had curvature of the spine, his loins and buttocks were numb, he was welded to the old-fashioned vinyl seat and knew he would never recover. Beside him, Mavis's flamboyant red hair drooped. Neither cared about anything any more, apart from the one persistant worry.

"Should we phone the police about the gas?"

"The house has probably blown up by now." It was difficult to speak, his larynx was comatose.

Lights were suddenly switched on inside the coach. "Flag-staff . . . We'll shortly be arriving in Flagstaff. Make sure you take everything with you."

They stumbled zombie-like on to the tarmac. Mr Pringle saw a doorway and wandered inside, brandishing his hotel voucher at yet another clerk. "Day's Inn."

"Sure, that's round the corner. On route 66. You want a cab?"

"There's . . ." and he indicated helplessly his five responsibilities.

"OK, you want two cabs? There's the phone, help yourself." But he could no longer read the figures on the card. The clerk took his coins and punched up the number.

"Hi. Two cabs to the dog kennel soon as you can."

It was a motel. Not glamorous. A utilitarian two-storey flimsy

34

set of rooms, temporary resting places, overlooking a car-park. The foyer was strewn with dust sheets and ladders, an indication that renovations might be in progress. The reception desk was manned by a student who raised reluctant eyes from his book.

"You got a reservation?"

"Five rooms." These might be the last words his parched lips would utter; Mr Pringle was ready to die in his bed.

"Oh, sure. Pringle and party."

As he led them up the outside staircase, the student observed curiously, "You folks look bushed. Where've you come from?"

"Gatwick," Ivor replied tersely, "by bus. It's all been a ghastly mistake."

Each room was identical. Jed Pointer gazed at his in disgust. After such a journey he lacked the energy to smash a single chair.

"Thousands of miles and we end up in a dump like this," he snarled.

Ivor Henry hobbled past to the room next door. "Nobody try and wake me or I'll kill them."

Monica Moffat said simply, "Good-night," and disappeared. Mr Pringle waited until Clarissa thing had pouted and shut her door before following Mavis into the last room of the row. As a gesture, the student drew the curtains and switched on the bedside lights.

"You look terrible. Sure you're OK?"

Mr Pringle's lips moved but this time no sound emerged.

"We're all right," Mavis said quickly. "We've had a bit of a long day."

His garments dropped to the floor of their own accord. Mavis eased off his shoes and pushed him between the creased yellow sheets.

"I bought a new nightie for this trip," she grumbled. "Dark blue chiffon with lace inserts. It wasn't worth it."

He sensed rather than saw her get into the adjoining bed and switch off the lights. His responsibility was finally at an end. Thankfully, Mr Pringle closed his eyes. He felt detached from his body. A great wave of nothingness swept over him and he embraced it like death.

The telephone brought him alive with a scream.

"Hi, Pringle? Dulce. You all arrived OK?"

"Aah . . . aah . . . !"

"That's great. I'll be arriving first thing in the morning with the crew. You had a good trip."

"Aah."

"Fine. See you at 7.00 a.m. Oh, and Pringle – "

"Heee . . ."

"Sleep well."

Chapter Three

Friday 16th

In the vast Las Vegas ballroom preparations were at full stretch.
A town which never slept, dedicated to extracting every cent,
had applied itself with equal fervour to the task of raising cash for
charity.

They intended everyone should know about it; as well as
transmitting the event, Las Vegas had extended pressing invitations for news coverage. As a result – the event itself, a record of
the event, potted biographies of everyone taking part, even
descriptions of wives, or better still, bimbos – no possible angle
had been ignored. The town overflowed, technicians had to be
squeezed in as well as the tourists, it was boom time.

Old hands grumbled it was worse than a Republican conven-
tion. Journalists stood ten deep in every bar, crews were having
to wait. An emergency was declared when the ice machine broke
down.

Outside, in desert heat, ordinary people were gathering,
sweltering along the Strip in front of the pink and blue of Caesar's
Palace, the gold and white of the glittering Pavilion and the lofty
scalloped shape of the Sands.

On the sidewalk in front of the golden, glass-fronted Château
des Beaux Rêves, there was a solid phalanx craning to see beyond
the garden with its fountains and palms. For the watchers, it was
enough to glimpse the favoured ones walking to and fro, to feel a
part of it.

Gamblers were protected from the crush. Above the crowds,
on moving walkways under a transparent air-conditioned car-
apace, a continuous worm, mainly of grey-suited Japanese, was
fed into the welcoming arms of the croupiers.

All along the Strip, those desirous of their fifteen minutes of fame were waiting in hotel rooms for agents to ring and confirm they'd been booked to appear with Frank. If only they could tell him (and the rest of the world) how much their hearts were bleeding for those poor deprived kids as well as mentioning their latest single (RT two minutes forty-seven seconds).

In subterranean suites, editors were being directed which film footage to include: "Five seconds of that Cambodian kid with no arms, OK? Three . . . two . . . one . . . that's enough. A few feet of that Ethiopian baby covered in flies . . . and the Indian leper who looks so cute. Not him, for Chrissake! I don't care if he is dying, we want people to give, not throw up."

In casino kitchens mounds of delicacies were being prepared to tempt sated appetites for it was clearly understood that those about to give could not be persuaded to excel on an empty stomach.

A lighting gantry had been erected above the ballroom. Lilliputian men manoeuvred spotlights into position, others pressed command buttons which raised or lowered the beams. When these were switched on, the demand would be enormous but even that had been allowed for and extra generators provided.

In a marquee the various components of the golden dish remained shrouded in plastic. This was to be assembled in the final hours before the junketing began, to keep its mechanics secret: most guarded of all was the code which, when tapped into the computer, allowed money to flow through into the containers below.

When full these boxes would travel in an armoured van, to the bank. All along the Strip this motorcade would be venerated by the crowds on the sidewalks whilst over their heads a vast firework display would blaze in the desert sky.

Afterwards, almost as an anticlimax, the money would be redistributed among charitable organisations who best knew the needs of the children themselves.

Watching every step would be armed security guards, hundreds of them ready to deal with any who might feel tempted to intervene. And in a special tented headquarters, state police were running checks on the whereabouts of all those who came into that category. This appeal was the Big One and Nevada took its responsibilities seriously.

*

Dawn broke on the sixteenth. The most important event today was the rehearsal, using stand-ins. By tonight, technicians promised one another with fingers crossed, any problems would be resolved. All those satellite dishes, radio links and the rest of the micro-technology would meld into a glorious whole. If not, someone else would be to blame. At present they were eager to finish the day's work and rub shoulders with the rest of the punters in this earthly illusion of paradise.

In a luxurious penthouse, a quiet voice informed room service that Mr Sinatra was ready for his coffee. On other phones, minions were making contact with their opposite numbers in London, Moscow and Tokyo. Mr Sinatra wanted a friendly chat with all of them before the synthetic bonhomie of show business took over.

As she watched the dawn from her verandah, Shirley decided it was as good a day as any to go into town and bank the money. In his room, Sammy grumbled to Bomber; he should have kept a few dollars back to have a good time with Charlene. She'd told him how much she wanted to go to Vegas. "If Mr Kuminsky comes, I'm going to ask him. A hundred dollars don't mean *nuthin'* to a man like Mr Kuminsky." Bomber thumped his tail in agreement. Somehow, Sammy couldn't see himself asking the same of Mr Freeman. There was something about Mr Freeman that meant you didn't ask for favours.

In the shabby motel room in Flagstaff, Mavis Bignell wondered whether her friend Mrs Ellis had achieved her objective.

And jammed among those thousands in Las Vegas, Mrs Ellis told her grandson she wasn't giving up her bit of pavement to anyone. Today promised to be as exciting as the last royal wedding. She'd come a long way to enjoy herself and provided her feet didn't give out, she'd stay till the end.

The thing was, as Mrs Bignell pointed out, you couldn't go on being cross with Mr Dulce even if he had, unbeknownst to everyone, arranged a 7.00 a.m. call. He wanted to make his film so they mustn't grumble if he expected them to work. It was obvious he wanted to make amends. Hadn't he turned up with bourbon for the men and bouquets for Monica, Clarissa thing and herself? People, Mrs Bignell said heavily, didn't often think to give other people flowers nowadays.

Anyway, despite so little sleep, they were feeling better, she claimed; it must be the dry Arizona air. This breakfast place was a novelty too; lovely fresh fruit and something extraordinary called hash brownies. Personally, she was looking forward to the filming. The crew who'd arrived in those big vans seemed pleasant enough although not very talkative.

Mr Pringle listened with half an ear. His body ached. Mavis was bright eyed and bushy tailed whereas he . . . He felt indignant: age had nothing to do with it, surely?

He had been expecting a showdown. To his astonishment thespian anger had evaporated. When Dulce arrived, Jed resisted longer than most but even he succumbed after the gift of whisky. Now the actors were in a huddle, listening intently as Dulce described the opening shots. One of the vans towed a make-up/wardrobe caravan and into this Jed and Clarissa disappeared.

Monica Moffat came towards them, coffee in hand and something half concealed by her handbag in the other. "May I . . . ?" Mr Pringle pulled out a chair and she gave him a charming smile. "I'm not needed in the first few set-ups. I shall go and have another snooze. I didn't sleep very well despite being tired."

Mavis was sympathetic. "It's not knowing whether it's night or day."

Mr Pringle checked his watch. "It's Friday the sixteenth. Whether a.m. or p.m. I'm not altogether sure."

"Ta, dear. You should get your head down while you can, Monica. You've got a lot to do once they reach your scenes."

"You've read the script?"

"I thought it was lovely." Mavis turned to Mr Pringle. "It's about this woman who tries to stop her daughter marrying this no-good boy. On the way she accidentally bumps into her own lost love. I won't tell you how it finishes, then it'll be a surprise, but I shall cry when I see it, I know I shall." Mr Pringle grunted.

"I wish I didn't have to carry this about with me." Monica put the object on the table. Mavis was fascinated.

"That's the gun you use when you . . . "

Monica nodded. "In the scene when Ivor and I have a showdown with Jed."

"Looks real, doesn't it?" Mr Pringle picked it up, mildly interested.

"It's a prop, of course."

"I've never handled one, real or otherwise . . . " He peered down the barrel.

Mavis uttered a squeak, "Careful!"

Inside the camera vehicle, Louis Carlson noticed. He spoke to the camera assistant, "Got the stills camera?"

"Sure."

"Quick, grab one of this." The camera assistant, discreetly hidden, adjusted the telephoto lens. Louis began fidgeting, "Hurry . . . hurry!"

"Don't rock the boat."

"See you get a clean one of him."

"I know!" The assistant was impatient now, "C'm on, c'm on, baby . . . That's better!" The motor drive whirred as Mr Pringle leaned back and squinted along the barrel. "Attaboy! One or two there you can use, I'd say."

"Great! Get them printed up."

"Hey, you want one of her as well?"

Louis peeped out cautiously. Mavis Bignell now had the pistol and was doing her version of Annie Oakley.

"Why not?" The camera clicked again. "Wait till she's acting tough . . . Like – now."

Back at the table, Monica Moffat was tucking the toy away in her bag. "At least it's not as heavy as a real one."

"Have we any information as to the schedule?" asked Mr Pringle. "I haven't had a chance to speak to Dulce yet."

"He's given us the shooting order. We're doing the motel scenes first; that's why we came here. He's arranged to use this as a location."

"Why on earth didn't he say so before?" Mr Pringle was irritated but Monica obviously didn't think it important.

"It's been such a rush, maybe he forgot."

"Or maybe he didn't want us to know about that long journey," Mavis observed shrewdly. "I don't suppose friend Jed would have agreed if he'd known."

"Nor would I have done," said Mr Pringle with feeling. "So how long *do* we stay here?"

Monica pulled a face. "Don't bother to unpack. We're due to finish the motel stuff by this evening then move on to Boulder City. It sounds pretty tight to me but Enrico was determined.

Once we arrive in Boulder we film there with Jed and Clarissa, stay overnight and do daylight scenes with them in the morning. Then we drive to Las Vegas. My encounter scene with Ivor is going to be shot on the actual Strip itself."

Mavis's eyes sparkled. "Isn't that marvellous – we'll be there on the Big Day – what a bit of luck! What time do we arrive?"

"Depends how quickly we finish at Boulder. Not until late tomorrow afternoon, I should think."

Nothing could spoil Mrs Bignell's joy.

"We'll get there in time, I can feel it in my bones."

"To see Mrs Ellis?"

"Oh, blow Mrs Ellis, dear, I can see her any day of the week. No, I meant Frank Sinatra."

It must be the food, Mr Pringle decided; Mrs Bignell wasn't usually fickle.

The crew began setting up the camera dolly to do shots of Jed and Clarissa arriving at the motel. Enrico Dulce came across.

"Monica, we need to do a colour check; could you let wardrobe see your costumes." When she'd gone, he said, "Pringle, can I ask you a great favour?"

"Certainly."

"Could you and Mavis go ahead to Boulder City and check the hotel? I can take care of everything here."

Not another ride on a greyhound bus his body protested but perhaps Dulce guessed. "Hire yourself a decent car, do it in style," he ordered. "Hell, you two weren't expecting that long haul yesterday." Neither was anyone else; Mr Pringle was confused.

Dulce was waving yet more dollars plus an address. "Here's where we're due to stay and that's five hundred to take care of additional expenses. It should be a nice drive. Take it easy. Enjoy! Fix it so you can leave the car in Vegas, OK? Oh, and settle the motel bill here, would you? We'll be checking out after lunch."

Without waiting for an answer he strode away. Mr Pringle was stunned but Mavis shook her head in admiration.

"That's the film business for you, all get-up-and-go."

"Driving was not part of our agreement," Mr Pringle said stiffly. "Besides, they may not accept an English driving licence."

"Of course they will," Mavis cried happily. "Come on, let's find a pretty limo."

*

In the communications room at the Beaux Rêves, the temporary operator, Judy Beeker, glanced at her watch. She was a frail, fair-haired woman in her mid-forties. Today she was terrified. She'd managed so far but the worst part was still to come; if only her hands would stop shaking, maybe she could do the rest. When the minute hand was exactly at five past the hour, she suddenly dabbed at her face and pretended to be in distress. "God, I feel dizzy."

"You want some water?" asked the staff girl. "There's a fountain at the end of the hall."

"Could you . . . I don't think I can make it that far."

As the door closed, Judy was on her feet. She took a spindly looking key from her purse and fiddled with the lock of the relay store. Hurry, hurry! She had to change over two of the breakers, Del Freeman had shown her how. He and the nameless blind man had made her practise until she could do it in less than a minute but this was for real; she fumbled. The door wouldn't open! She tugged and finally it worked. Quickly! The relays clicked into position. She regained her seat and dialled. Ozal answered, "Yes?"

"Ready." She gripped the table; a lonely widow whose drug-addicted son had been kept out of jail, at a price. It was a mystery how the blind man came to know so much. Del Freeman had scared her more, though. Scott had been allowed to escape, hadn't he? Freeman demanded. He'd slipped bail and disappeared; the Family had given her the money for the fine.

She'd nodded, desperately wanting to ask if she'd ever see Scott again, but she'd been too frightened. Maybe now that she'd done what they wanted? They'd warned her never to speak of it, they needn't have bothered; she was too terrified.

The regular telephonist re-entered. "Feeling better?"

"A little." Judy sipped, her eyes flicking again at her wrist. In forty-three minutes she would have to think of another excuse.

"I'm bringing a TV with me tomorrow," the regular girl told her in friendly fashion. "I've never seen Frankie in the flesh, have you?"

Judy Beeker forced herself to sound calm and interested. "No, no I haven't."

43

Forty-one minutes. Tomorrow she would put as many miles as possible between herself and Las Vegas.

Gino stared in the mirror. When your features were as regularly Italian as his were, you had to add something for people to remember. To distract Sammy it had been a different hair parting and an ornate gold medallion. Today he'd added a sickle scar above his left eyebrow, plus a coin in his shoe. He'd also curled his hair, using Myra's tongs. No longer sleek, he looked more Greek than Italian.

He hadn't revealed his changed appearance to the others; it was an extra he and Myra had worked out. A precaution that his secretive nature required. She had changed over the photograph in his pass, stamping the numbers so that it would take a careful examination to notice. Myra was clever like that, a gift of a wife.

Gino examined his reflection again. Curls were the final touch, he doubted whether John or Louis would recognise him immediately now. Not that they would have the chance, his role was separate. It might not be a complete disguise but it was sufficient to give him a breathing space, should he need one.

As he drove he allowed himself to wonder about Louis. Myra had worried him. During their daily phone call, she'd been insistent, "It's too big for Louis to handle, Gino. If he panics, that's it. You're far too visible in this whole thing."

"Maybe."

"Talk to Ozal," she begged, "let him know how we feel."

"Louis is my friend, Myra . . . " In the pause, Gino heard her hang up. Betrayal didn't come easily to either of them. All the same . . . Gino Millar had no intention of going down with a loser.

He parked his truck outside one of the rear entrances to the Beaux Rêves and went through two security checks without difficulty. Outside the power house the guard read the name on the pass.

"Kuminsky?"

"Maintenance."

He ran expert hands over Gino. "Let's see inside the bag." Gino held it open and the guard glanced briefly at the contents. "What's the problem?"

"Stand-by generators. One of 'em's running hot."

"OK." The guard punched four digits on his handset. Ozal answered.

"Service department."

"Power room. A guy called Kuminsky . . ?"

"Oh, sure. We've got a surge. Nothing serious but he'll have to isolate the rest while he's working on the hot one."

"Thanks." He stood aside to let Gino pass. "How long?" Gino appeared to consider.

"Half an hour, maybe three-quarters."

Watched by the guard, he limped along the line of machinery. Out of sight, he slipped off the shoe and peeled back the inner sole. Beneath were six cut-out devices, each smaller than a finger nail. Gino moved to the first generator.

As soon as the last was in position, he went to the wall phone and let the service number ring twice. The guard reappeared.

"I was letting them know upstairs."

"Uh-huh." The man indicated the limp as Gino gathered up his tools. "Nam?"

"Yeah."

"Too bad."

In his room Ozal used a radio transmitter. Three miles away in the desert, one of Gino's team heard the signal and said, "That's it. Wagons roll." In the communications room, the minute hand jerked forward. Judy almost sagged with relief. Only two more things to do then it was finished.

"I'm feeling fine now," she told the staff girl, "so if you'd like to take an early lunch . . . "

In the special tented headquarters the security firm had set up in the desert, the patrol chief examined the revised list of drivers.

"Changes, Freeman?"

"One had already requested vacation, sir. The other guy bust a foot cleaning his wife's car," said John Millar.

"How the hell he do that?"

John gave him a thin smile. "Left the brake off. Car slid over his toes."

"Son-of-a-bitch – and him an ex-cop? We'll need to run checks on these new names – " but John had already moved to the computer keyboard.

"Allow me." He tapped rapidly. "Ready for you now, sir."

The chief heaved his beer belly upright, lumbered across and scanned the screen.

"Looks satisfactory." He initialled the form, "OK, Freeman, go ahead and issue the paperwork."

"Thank you, sir."

Boulder City reduced Mavis Bignell to a gasp. In the driving seat, Mr Pringle relaxed with eyes closed. The E-Z parking lot had proved anything but.

"Will you look at that!" she demanded. "Isn't it amazing!"

"I'd rather not."

"It's incredible."

It was early evening. Reflected in the waters of the Colorado river, an enormous showboat blazed with light. "It's a gambling joint," Mavis said delightedly. "It's not a boat at all."

"They're all gambling joints." Her companion was tetchy. "I've never experienced anything like it. At every bus-stop, every village. Even that café in Searchlight where we tried to get a cup of tea . . . that woman, suckling her infant while she played *chemin de fer*, it was obscene."

It might have seemed to him depravity but Mavis said nonchalantly, "It wasn't a café, it was a casino. They don't seem to go in for tea rooms out here. It reminded me of a club Herbert once took me to in Blackpool." Mr Pringle muttered something under his breath and she responded sharply, "I'm not likely to forget the occasion, dear. He didn't take me away that often and it was where he gambled five quid and lost the lot. We'd better see if we can find Mr Dulce's hotel."

"How?"

"Ask a policeman, of course."

Mr Pringle struggled out of his seat-belt. "Let's see if we can find one without a gun; they make me twitchy."

Louis Carlson was in a seventh heaven all of his own. How often had he dreamed of becoming a film director? Now his dreams had come true even if the circumstances were phoney. He'd coaxed good performances out of the actors – hell, that was part of the plan; convincing them he was genuine.

Finally he announced, "OK, that's a wrap for today." The

assistant reached up to switch off the lights. Around the motel room, actors collapsed like puppets.

"I can't remember when I've ever felt so tired," whimpered Clarissa.

Monica agreed. "I trust we're not going to keep up this pace."

"Sorry, sweetheart." There were dark patches under her eyes which make-up couldn't conceal. "Maybe I've pushed you a little too hard," Louis soothed. "Take a shower, get changed. We'll have a snack here in Flagstaff, then be on our way. Pringle's gone ahead to check the rooms so when you arrive, you and Ivor can just roll into bed. The kids have got a couple more set-ups. OK Clarissa? Just two simple shots, that's all. We'll do the rest in the morning. It won't be such a tough day tomorrow, I promise."

The assistants were clearing away the equipment and he went outside to the film truck. In the truck the "cameraman" was one of Ozal's lieutenants. Now for a little acting of his own, thought Louis.

"I wish I could rely on that Pringle guy."

"You told him what to do?"

"Yeah, but he's so dumb." Louis feigned even greater unease. "I'd like to check for myself. Can you take over for me here?" The cameraman's gaze was steady; altering any part of the plan wasn't in the book.

"Call Ozal. Make sure he says yes."

"Sure," Louis said easily.

Twenty minutes later he tapped on the door of the truck. Someone turned a key and he slipped inside. The cameraman and soundman were trying on the uniforms they would wear tomorrow night.

"Ozal agrees," Louis said simply. "You follow with the Brits, OK?"

"Where will we meet?"

"In Boulder City, at the hotel. Ozal's asked me to check a coupla other things first."

"But we will see you around?" the cameraman asked deliberately.

"Sure." Louis tried to sound genial. "And it's going great. Those four will have tears in their eyes when they tell the cops what a beautiful film we're making."

"All the same, you've got a problem, Carlson."

"Oh?"

"That hooch you gave 'em," drawled the soundman, "the young limey actor told us he was aiming to finish his bottle tonight."

"Shit!" Jed's performance was needed in Vegas, not here. Ozal's men were watching him.

"OK, I'll handle it."

Louis bounded up the outside staircase, his mind working feverishly. Ten minutes, that's all. He daren't arrive too late in Boulder City and he needed time to locate the ranch. He'd listened to Gino attentively but he'd only managed to snatch a glimpse of John's airmap in New York. "Hi, Jed. There's something I want you to know."

There was another alteration which Ozal hadn't sanctioned; this time John Millar was responsible. He had already decided to act on his own and not to tell Ozal. There was no chance of it being discovered for days, so why fret? He had to justify it to himself, though: it was extra insurance.

As he drove down the quiet, slightly sleazy, street, John wondered if his journey would prove unnecessary. Judy Beeker might have left town already; if she'd any sense she would have gone. John found himself hoping she would still be here, it made him feel excited. He waited in the shadows until the street was empty before pressing the buzzer.

"Yes?"

That settled it. She was stupid, she might even be about to tell someone. Justification for what he was about to do was swift. John murmured into the entryphone.

"Del Freeman."

"Oh . . . Just a minute."

It was the sight of his uniform which surprised her into holding open the apartment door.

"I didn't realise you were in the police?"

He knew the layout from the previous visit. Through the arch, he saw the open suitcase on the bed. It was going to be so easy! As she saw his face, Judy Beeker had a sudden premonition; she stared with terrified eyes and made a last pathetic attempt at an appeal.

"I'm leaving . . . soon as I'm packed. My sister's in Little Rock, I can stay there for as long as I like."

She'd freshened her lipstick but she hadn't used a mirror. Her lips were a scarlet smudged circle. He needed her to drop her guard, just for a second.

"How did it go today?"

"Oh, fine. I put the breaker back and fixed it to the wall, no one suspected a thing. Listen, you're not going to ask me to . . . Oh, no. No thanks."

She was warding off the dollars. "Look, Mr Freeman, I don't want any money. I don't want to be involved any more, that's all. Please!"

Had she taken it, he could have been more efficient. As it was, she had time to cry out before he got close enough to silence her.

Ivor Henry heard the altercation in the next room. When Dulce slammed the door he returned to his lines. It took longer to commit words to memory these days and in twenty minutes they were due to leave. There was another interruption. "Yes, what is it?" Jed entered uninvited and slumped into a chair. "Pointer, I'm busy."

"What d'you know about Dulce?" Ivor looked blank. "I mean, do you know *anything* about this film set-up?"

"Only what Avril told us, why?"

"Did you ever see such a minimal crew? And where were the cutaways, reaction shots and stuff? He just went hell for leather, one shot per page."

Oh-ho, thought Ivor, someone's little ego is deflated because he didn't have any close-ups!

"I believe the style's known as drama-doc. They're using super sixteen so they don't need extra lights. These days, the grammar of filming has changed, you know – "

"Bollocks! There's something bloody odd, in case you hadn't noticed."

"Pointer, if Dulce told you not to get drunk, there's nothing odd about that. Personally, I whole-heartedly approve – "

"He's taken away the bottle, OK? It was the *way* he did that which I didn't like. Up to now he's been an easygoin' sort of geezer, know what I mean?"

"He's efficient," Ivor said slowly. "He doesn't waste time, I wouldn't describe that as easygoing."

"He didn't come the heavy though, did he?"

"So?"

"He almost broke my bleeding arm, grabbing that bottle. It still hurts."

"That must have been a shock."

"Don't you bloody laugh, mate! I'm used to looking after myself."

"I wasn't laughing."

"Last bloke pulled a trick like that, he'd been in the marines."

"It's a rough tough country over here."

"I wouldn't like to *cross* friend Dulce, straight up."

He left and Ivor brooded; if Dulce had put the fear of God into Jed, so much the better. But as he picked up his suitcase, Ivor had a momentary doubt as to whether Dulce was genuine.

Sammy was firing his air rifle at a Coke tin balanced on a post. His grandma warned him she'd be away all day. He'd asked if he could tag along but she'd said no. She'd left instructions what to do about food. She'd shouted at him to remember to feed the stock. He'd done all that. He'd tried to teach Bomber a new trick but the dog was bored, too. They were both stuck here because Grandma had taken the pick-up.

There was a noise. Bomber's ears pricked up. It wasn't a helicopter this time, it was a car approaching down the long track that led from the highway. In it he could see Charlene and some of the hands from the next-door ranch. "Hi! Hi, Charlene!" He bounced up and down with excitement and one of the hands jeered.

"Cut that out." Charlene had baby blonde hair tied in a blue ribbon to match her eyes. She wore a gingham frock with nothing beneath except her pants. You could tell that when the wind blew. The breeze did that now, billowing the thin cotton as she got out.

"Hi, Charlene," Sammy said again.

"We're aiming to go to Boulder City. You got any money Sammy?"

"No, but I'd sure like to come."

"Can't you ask your grandma?"

"She's out."

There was a discussion then one of the hands said pointedly, "Ain't there no money anywhere in the house?"

"Not a cent," said Sammy proudly. "Grandma took it all."

"Not much use you coming then."

"Aw, let him," Charlene shrugged. "He makes me laugh. Go put your best jeans on, Sammy." The boy yelled excitedly, dashed inside and within minutes had re-emerged, pulling up his zip and tripping over Bomber who romped round his feet.

"Stay there. Good dog." Sammy dived into the back of the car which was already on the move.

"You ain't bothered to lock up, Sam?"

"Bomber's guarding the place." The hand looked back at the disconsolate mutt.

"Don't much look like it to me."

"When you think about it, all this gambling is like bingo only more glamorous," Mavis said happily. "But I think I've had enough for the time being, thank you."

They'd found the hotel without difficulty. The surprise had been to discover the booking was again in the name of Pringle.

"We were told these five rooms are wanted later today. You saying you need them now, or what?" the clerk had demanded impatiently.

"We'd like to see one now, that's all," Mavis explained, "and Mr Dulce asked us to make sure the other four were in order. Are they all quite comfortable?" She might have been speaking Chinese.

"Lady, a room is a room is a room. You want yours ahead of schedule? Could you wait, please, while I check with room service?"

She and Mr Pringle moved away from the desk. "I expect it'll be all right. I mean, if they're all identical."

"If so, I can't quite see why we were asked to come. And I am a little puzzled at the constant use of my name. We only met the man two days before we left."

Mavis pondered. "They are very efficient, the Americans. You saw what it was like this morning. You are the company manager. Mr Dulce must have told his office to use your name when they made the reservations." She frowned. "As it's only five rooms, I wonder where he and the crew are planning to stay?"

"That, I'm thankful to say, is not my concern."

"Well, then," she was cheerful again, "we've done what he asked. Once we've unpacked, the next thing is to enjoy ourselves, remember." He caught the gleam in her eye and his heart sank.

"No, Mavis."

"You've got that extra five hundred dollars."

"That was for additional expenses."

"Gambling is expenses," she insisted, "in Nevada. All there is to spend your money on are fruit machines, casinos or marriage parlours – and you know my views about those – so we really haven't any choice. Have we?"

If only she hadn't got the hang of it so quickly. Mr Pringle followed glumly, doing his best to check her excesses. "Mavis, that yellow counter is worth £5.46 at today's rate of exchange!"

"I do wish you'd put your calculator away, dear. Relax. And could you change these blue ones for me. I want to try the fruit machines. They look more interesting than the one at the Bricklayers. Oh, look . . . "

Inevitably, on the television screen came more promotional material for the charity appeal; this time, of the rehearsal.

"They're making quite a thing of it, aren't they? I'm so glad we'll be there."

"It would be more convenient to watch from a hotel room," he suggested, "cooler and far more comfortable."

"Not on your nelly, dear. Monica said Mr Dulce intends to film a scene with her and Ivor right outside where they're doing the appeal . . . and I'm going to be there. You never know, Frank Sinatra might appear on a balcony, like the Queen."

When she was on a winning streak and had the equivalent of £17.97 profit, Mrs Bignell graciously agreed to stop. "I'm sure Mr Dulce would want us to have a slap-up meal to round off our day. You can have this towards it," she offered her winnings. Mr Pringle discovered he was hungry.

"We don't know when the others will arrive, so we might as well," he agreed. "However, I couldn't face any more hamburgers."

"Neither could I. Somewhere posh, with wine. We'll find a place, book a table, then go back and get changed."

They were wandering along, examining menus on display when Mavis heard the Lancashire accent.

"Damn and blast!"

"Well, well, well. You must be from England?"

Shirley Callaghan turned to find a plump, friendly-looking, red-head standing there.

"A long time ago I was."

"You got a problem?"

"It's my old pick-up. I think it's gone and died."

"May I be of assistance?" Shirley saw flannel trousers, tweed jacket, viyella shirt and woolly pullover topped by an ancient panama.

"You've got to be British," she said. The man brushed a hand over his moustache and raised his hat.

"How very perspicacious. Pringle, G D H," he said, gratified, "and my friend, Mrs Mavis Bignell. Shall I see what I can do?"

Mavis knew it was doomed to fail. She didn't interfere, she didn't want to hurt his feelings, but engines always had been a problem; they never seemed to co-operate. His old Allegro was the only one that did but this was an ancient Ford.

"It's not going to go, I'm afraid," Mr Pringle admitted finally.

Shirley sighed. "You're right. Next problem is, how do I get home? Not that you two need worry," she added hastily.

"How about eating first?" suggested Mavis. "We were just about to, weren't we, dear, and we'd be glad if you'd join us. Mr Dulce's standing us a treat and I'm adding my winnings, so we're in funds."

Mr Pringle raised his hat once more, "We'd be honoured, in fact."

"And why don't we take you home afterwards? We've got this great big hire car and it's doing nothing but sit in the parking lot." He shuddered at the thought of journeying along dark foreign roads but rallied courteously.

"The obvious solution. Please accept our offer."

Shirley looked from one to another.

"This is my lucky day. Tell you what, when we get back to the ranch, I can offer a decent cuppa tea."

"Now you're talking," said Mrs Bignell.

Chapter Four

Later on the 16th

The old woman from the downstairs apartment had been on the lookout. She had followed the two patrolmen up to the first floor and now stood in the doorway to watch them search. "I'm certain I never saw her leave."

"Well, I can't see her anywhere, can you?" In the kitchen recess, the first officer rattled the handle of a door which led on to a fire-escape.

"Judy always keeps that locked," she told him. "We all do. This neighbourhood is full of Hispanics. Used to be only *decent* people lived round here."

"Maybe she went away without telling you for once?"

"She always stops by to ask me to collect her mail and water her plants, things like that. Everyone does. I can't get out so that's how I repay for when they go to the grocery store. I phoned her sister in Little Rock after I called you – she's the only person Judy ever visits. She wasn't expecting her."

"OK." The second officer was bored. He moved beyond the arch to the bed, knocking over a chair. "Shit! Look, lady, you can see for yourself your friend's not here." His colleague had opened the closet and clothes tumbled out, bringing with them the smells of their owner and her stale perfume. The old woman showed disapproval as he bundled them back.

"There was her son, Scott," she told him. "He took drugs. When he disappeared, that's when Judy moved in here. She was always hoping he'd call but he never did."

Next to the closet were two deep drawers. The bottom one wasn't quite shut and the second officer pushed at it with his foot.

"Got an address?"

"He jumped bail. No one knows where he went after that.

Broke her heart."

One end of the drawer remained jammed open. The officer bent down to jerk at the handle impatiently. The drawer slid forward a few inches. He seemed not to hear what the woman had just said.

"Where's the phone?" he rasped.

"Over here, by the door."

He rose, arms akimbo to block her view as he walked the few steps to where she stood.

"OK, lady. We'll be down to talk to you about Scott. Got to make a few calls first." The truth reached her. She tried to find a trace of hope in his eyes, delaying the horror as long as possible.

"I heard her. Judy must have been alive because I heard her cry out."

"In a little while," he promised. "Go back down and wait for us, OK?" The old woman reached out for support and found a chair back.

"It wasn't Scott . . . couldn't have been. She always said how close they were." Frail shoulders were hunched against evil as she moved off towards the elevator. The patrolman was concerned enough to watch and see she didn't fall. Then she remembered something. "Hey, there were two men here a few weeks back. I only saw them leave. She wouldn't say why they'd called – I thought it must be about Scott. One was blind."

The rehearsals were over and the great ballroom was dim. Cleaners moved slowly; they were paid by the hour so why sweat. The air-conditioning had been turned to maximum to freshen the place before the twelve-hour marathon began. In the gallery, the lighting director made a few last-minute changes, his assistant programmed them into the console. Above on the gantry, two maintenance hands were checking the circuitry. One had a scar, dark curly hair and a limp.

"OK to switch off up here?" he called out.

"Yeah, we're finished."

From his bird's eye position, Gino waited until the gallery was empty before he and the power engineer set to work.

In the marquee, the golden bowl had been assembled. Representatives of the sponsors were having a demonstration.

"You see a perfect golden surface, gentlemen. As solid as it looks . . . " The designer hit the bowl several times to produce a ringing bell tone. "Once donations reach a certain height, roughly just above the level of the brim, we send a signal." He tapped the code on his control panel. "The cover slides over the top making a perfect sphere, two hatches in the base slide open . . . money falls through into the bullet-proof containers beneath."

"Any danger of any spilling out?"

"Take a look." They crouched to stare at the chute connected to the heavy box. "We aim not to lose one single cent, gentlemen."

"Fine."

"During the final hours of the appeal, our intention is to let the stack of money reach as high as possible, to encourage people to give even more. That's when there *is* a danger of dollars spilling over. What we plan is for armed guards to move forward and surround the bowl at that point. The entire area will be spot lit, with security cameras focused on any single thing that moves.

"I give you my word, gentlemen, not one cent will vanish. We owe it to those deprived kids."

There were appreciative murmurs. The designer indicated the control unit. "The code to operate this is known only to one other person besides myself. For safety reasons."

"I have a question?"

"Certainly."

"The bowl – it's a curve – what stops it tilting?"

"Can someone pass me the model?" This was handed to him and the designer showed how the bowl rested on a four-sided base. "*Voilà* . . . these supports fit the curve perfectly, therefore no problem."

"They also mask the containers?"

"Those will be below the level of the stage beneath where the bowl is situated. Additional security men will be on duty down there, of course. People want to see their contributions go in, followed by seeing their names on the screen. They're not interested in what happens after that. That's up to the banks and those of you who represent the charities, of course."

"First you see the money, then you don't," joked someone.

"Sir, I don't find that remark very funny," said the designer.

★

Louis drove with one eye on the map. He'd plotted the route the helicopter must have taken with John and Gino on board, glimpsed only briefly that day in New York, but the place had to be somewhere along this road, surely to God.

He'd talked to Beth. He couldn't get the conversation out of his mind, it was driving him crazy. He'd tried to insist she and the kids be ready to leave tomorrow midnight but Beth had refused. He'd put out of his mind the possibility that she would do that which was stupid. Beth always kept her word. She demanded he pull out now before it was too late. It was already far, far too late but she wouldn't accept that. She swore unless he pulled out, she'd never see him again.

"Never is too long, sweetheart," the phone felt like an instrument of torture. His hurt was reflected back at him in the dark glass of the windscreen. "Wait till you see all that money . . . you'll feel differently." This had made her mad.

She was furious at having to stay in the small narrow-minded house in Boston – he'd been counting on that – but now she only had one thing to say to him and kept repeating it, over and over: give up. The trouble was he didn't know how to make her change her mind.

He forced himself to concentrate. He'd made one other phone call, to the hotel in Boulder City, using the irate tones of a motel owner who'd been cheated. "You got a guy called Pringle? He gave this as his forwarding address."

"Let me check – "

"He's with a bunch of Brits. What I'm telling you is, no credit, OK? He fooled me and five rooms ain't chicken feed." He hung up before the manager could respond. Establish the dumbo all the way, Ozal said, draw attention to him. Louis had done his best.

The entrance to the ranch came up unexpectedly. He swung in a tight turn, dowsing his lights.

The moon was in its first quarter, shedding a mean glimmer on the rocky outcrop in the distance. He could barely make out the old barn Gino had described. Closer to was the homestead. The windows were dark. He'd planned what he was going to do: he would introduce himself to the old lady and charm her into trusting him and not Gino or John. After all, she'd be here after the money was dropped off. There were bound to be a thousand and one places where she could hide it and then disappear herself

57

for a while. He'd offer his protection. The others who were coming for the pay-out daren't hang around, they'd have to clear out. He could explain all this, plus the advantage of relying on him, she was bound to see it his way. All it depended on was charm, and the guts to see it through.

It had been different before; other people had given the orders. Ozal, for instance. When Ozal said go tell the man we're waiting for the protection money, all Louis had to do was lean on the guy. The sight of his huge frame was usually sufficient. The Family only protected small businesses, they didn't interfere with the big boys.

This time it would be OK because he didn't have to threaten anyone and Louis preferred it that way.

Maybe though, he ought to try and frighten her into trusting him? It all depended on what kind of old lady this one turned out to be. To give himself courage, Louis was carrying his gun tonight, as well as his knife. Tucked inside his belt, the hard cold shape gave him confidence. Cautiously, he released the clutch and his car began to trickle down the track.

Charlene's reason for wanting to go to Boulder was straightforward. "If we win, we can go to Vegas tomorrow. Go on, let Sammy have a try. Maybe he'll get lucky." One of the hands reluctantly handed over a five-dollar bill.

"It's a loan. See you give it me back, dick-head."

The chips were clammy in Sammy's hand. He made his choice, piled them all on his lucky number, closed his eyes and willed, and willed, until the wheel stopped turning. Charlene gasped.

"Hey, will you look at that! Come on, Sammy, do it again!"

Mr Pringle snoozed contentedly in the back of the hired limousine while Mrs Bignell chattered away to Shirley Callaghan. Mavis had a wonderful way, which he admired but couldn't imitate, of befriending a complete stranger in a matter of moments.

Tonight, by a tortuous route, she had discovered a connection between herself and Shirley through the late unlamented Herbert Bignell. As was his custom, Herbert had picked up one of his many ladyfriends on the dance floor of the King's Hall, Belle Vue.

"He never took *me* dancing after we were married," Mavis sighed, "he was too damn mean. When it came to his extra-marital activities, he usually stuck to the A1. He was a commercial, you see, he didn't often travel in the north west. I didn't know anything about the goings-on until he died. I'd had my suspicions – you'd have to be daft not to notice the little things – but he was a good liar, I'll give him that. I never caught him out. But once he was tucked up in the Co-op Chapel of Rest, I started going through his personal effects and I found this little address book. It was a shock when I realised . . . but I invited them all to the funeral."

"You never!"

Mavis chuckled. "Quite frankly, I was curious. And d'you know, several of 'em came. I was surprised."

"Not guilty," Shirley said firmly. "I was a one-man-girl after I'd met Cal."

"I'm sure you were, dear, but it's a small world, isn't it? What with you meeting your husband and Herbert finding someone at Belle Vue as well." She frowned. "You know, I don't think that one turned up . . . I'm sure I sent her an invite. It might have been the journey, of course, all the way from Manchester. To be quite honest, I can't even remember her name. It was a long time ago."

Mr Pringle was somnolent. He'd accepted Shirley's offer to drive and Mrs Bignell was supposed to be taking note of the route in between her chatter, to guide them back to Boulder City. It seemed simple enough to find, thank goodness.

"Here we are . . . where the yellow marker stones are."

"They show up well in the headlights, don't they?"

Shirley turned in along a dirt track between rail and post fencing. Despite the soft suspension, he noticed the potholes. Mr Pringle blinked himself awake and stared over Mavis's shoulder, curious to see his first all-American home.

"There's no light, Sammy must've gone to bed," Shirley exclaimed in surprise. "I hope he remembered to feed the stock." She had explained her grandson's deficiencies over dinner.

"Is that part of it, him being forgetful?" Mavis asked gently.

"He's not usually too bad." Shirley stared into the darkness, worried. "I can't hear Bomber, can you? He's normally making a racket when I get this far."

They pulled up in front of the wooden verandah. She got out, calling, "Hang on a minute" and went swiftly up the steps, pulling open the fly-screen. "You might trip up," she said as she reached for the switch, then, "oh, blast! The bulb must've gone. I'll fetch a torch, I won't be a minute. I can't think what's happened. Oh, my God!"

"What is it? What's the matter?" Mavis was hurrying up the steps, Mr Pringle at her heels, calling, "Is something wrong?"

In the darkness, a torch beam waved at them. A familiar voice hissed, "Get inside, all of you. Keep your hands where I can see them."

Simultaneously, Shirley reached for another switch and this time it worked. As the light came on, there was an explosion inside the room. Mavis screamed, then cried out in astonishment, "Mr Dulce! What on earth are you doing here . . . you've got a gun. Oh, Jesus, will you look at that poor dog!" Mr Pringle did, and immediately felt very, very poorly.

Tucked inside a camper on the outskirts of Las Vegas, Ozal was busy. He had two phones; one was the special line. When it rang, it was the cameraman on Louis's crew.

"It's Carlson, Ozal. We're in Boulder City as per the schedule. He went on ahead to do whatever it was you'd asked him to do. Now we're ready to start, only he's not here."

Ozal's brain raced.

"You got the right place?"

"Opposite the show boat, that's what he told us," the cameraman said uncertainly. "We've taken a look, there's no sign."

"You know the shots he wants?"

"Sure. Just the kids – "

"Get started," Ozal ordered. "Stick to the schedule. Start filming and keep filming until he turns up. Make sure plenty of people see what you're doing."

"Will do." The voice sounded relieved. "Thanks."

"Call me again if there's a problem, from the vehicle."

"That's where I am now." The cameraman said hesitantly, "Carlson seemed kinda nervous. That guy sweats like a pig, you know."

"It's his wife," Ozal said smoothly. "Louis is concerned about her, don't worry about it." He rang off, wondering what the hell Louis was up to.

Behind him, the television whispered out the weather and local news. The volume was low and he ignored it, he was too preoccupied.

On his car radio, John Millar heard the item. The body of part-time telephone operator Judy Beeker had been found doubled up in a drawer of her apartment; she had been strangled. He cursed from shock and fear; that wasn't how he'd planned it! The bitch might betray them after all. He hadn't intended the body be found until afterwards. How the hell had it happened? She was the loneliest woman on the block.

At headquarters, Homicide had taken over the investigation. The searches into Beeker's apartment had been made although all the results weren't in yet, the preliminary medical report was being typed up and it had been decided by the captain which information to release, which to withhold.

The public need not be told, for instance, that the police were interested in identifying the blind man and his accomplice. Not until computers sending messages across interstate boundaries had jogged one another's memory files.

In their second-floor office, Detective Lieutenant Gary Hocht and Detective Sergeant Rob Purcelle resumed comparing notes as soon as the news item finished. They had worked as a team many times. Neither was aggressive or fuelled by anger, both had been too long in the job for that. Results depended on efficiency and a willingness to undertake boring routine. They were dedicated to rendering the only possible service to their clients, that of identifying their killers, even if this meant hours of numbing questioning.

They had already interviewed the old woman who had described Judy Beeker's even pattern of existence. With her help they had built up a picture of her life during the last two weeks, both before and after the visit of the unknown men.

"Everything changes after that," the sergeant pointed out. "The following morning Beeker already knew there was a temporary vacancy at the Beaux Rêves when she rang her agency." He referred to his notes, "According to them Beeker stated she could do with the work and had heard on the grapevine someone had gone sick. She'd told the agency a fortnight previously that she might be visiting her sister and didn't want any work during that time."

"They booked her for two days but she only did one shift because she was murdered that same night."

"Assuming there is a connection, maybe she'd done what was necessary."

"Has to be a connection," Lieutenant Hocht protested. "Have we been able to contact the operator Beeker replaced?"

"She's on vacation. That too was sudden, apparently."

The lieutenant shrugged. "Part of the same picture." He pushed himself back from his desk and balanced his feet on a drawer. A tall, lanky man, uncomfortable in an office, but he had to be patient tonight; someone might call as a result of the news broadcast. "So, what did those two ask her to do? More important, what are they planning to do next?"

"And what the hell is a blind man doing in Vegas?"

"It's got to be the charity appeal," Hocht said flatly. Rob Purcelle sighed. At this morning's briefing they'd been told of the fourteen separate attempts, already identified, to get hold of that magic twenty-three million dollars.

"You would think none of those guys had children," he grumbled. "I mean, what type of a punk robs deprived kids?"

Hocht smiled faintly. "You still believe in the milk of human kindness, Rob?"

Purcelle flushed. "When it comes to kids . . . " he began and stopped. The lieutenant had no desire to embarrass him.

"It's what brings everyone to Vegas, let's face it," he said briskly. "It's a bigger pot of gold right now, that's all. Read me that description again."

"The blind one is about six foot, wore shades, athletic build, about sixty. Moves on the balls of his feet according to the old lady. She used to enjoy dancing so she looks out for that in a man. She thinks he was bald but wasn't sure. Probably too interested in his feet." Purcelle broke off from his notes. "There aren't any windows in the passage outside her apartment. She saw them coming out of the elevator and she was still wearing her reading glasses, that's why she didn't see too much detail."

"Uh-huh. She ain't done badly."

"His companion was a sharp dresser, slim, mid to late

twenties. Maybe they belong at the Beaux Rêves?"

The lieutenant shook his head. "They're pros, the strangler anyway. Nothing to stop a blind man doing that. The old lady said Beeker was the shy, nervous type. I wonder why she let him in?" He watched the printer in the corner spewing out continuous sheets of paper and sighed. "Looks like we got plenty more suspects. You know what worries me most?"

"What?"

"All the hired help. Those temporary 'security guards' every-where."

"They've all been given clearance."

"Oh, sure . . . " Hocht was sarcastic. "Would you bet your next rise none of 'em have a police record?"

"No."

"Exactly."

"But a blind guy isn't going to turn up in uniform carrying a gun!"

"Maybe not. He'll have friends, though. What time does that regular telephone operator start her shift, the one who worked with Mrs Beeker?"

The sergeant looked at his watch. "In a half-hour."

"Let's get over there. If that phone was going to ring it would have done so by now. Tell someone to listen out after the next bulletin." The lieutenant swung himself upright, eager to be gone. "Could you do something for me?"

"Sure?"

"Take Leroy round to the old lady." Leroy was over six foot and bald. "Get him to stand near the elevator and ask her what's different about him. Tell her to try and *imagine* he's white, OK."

He scribbled the word "coffee" on a scrap of paper and stuffed it in his pocket as a reminder. The old lady had made coffee for everyone who'd called that morning, there was no reason in the lieutenant's mind why she should be out of pocket.

Tension was increasing; at the Beaux Rêves the atmosphere was hysterical. Hocht and Purcelle eased their way through crowds in the foyer and established their credentials with house security. They sat down to wait, the laconic lieutenant viewing the bustle with a frown. "Why has it got to be this way?"

"Huh?"

"Those deprived kids shouldn't have to be grateful. Not for food and clothes for Chrissake. 'Do good by stealth', isn't that what it says?"

The regular operator came hurrying across. As they saw her face they knew she'd heard the news.

"It was on TV," the words tumbled out, "I was at my mother's – I recognised her picture. What happened? I mean, why Judy? She was a nice, ordinary person." The lieutenant guided her into a quiet corner.

"Can you tell us anything about her? Did she talk much that day?"

"I'd never met her before, she wasn't the usual one from the agency. We were busy, especially so because of . . . all this," she indicated the crowds. "Judy was on time. She introduced herself. We were pretty busy. She was quiet, sort of sad looking, maybe because she wasn't feeling all that well."

"Oh?"

"Mid–morning she said she felt faint. I got her some water. She was fine after that."

"How long were you gone?"

"Gone?" Her eyebrows went up. "The faucet's only at the end of the hall."

"Can you show us exactly what you did."

Up on the first floor, the girl went through the motions while the sergeant timed it. As she reached the door of the communications room, he looked up. "Three and a half minutes."

"OK. Is that how it was, Miss?"

"Yes. The reason it took longer was because I had to load a fresh tube of paper cups."

"Can we go inside and would you show me what you can do in that room in three and a half minutes?"

The girl's eyes widened. "I don't know. Call long distance, call the moon if there's anyone up there these days."

They followed her, crowding into the space behind the switchboards where two other operators were working. The lieutenant spotted the wall cupboard immediately.

"What's inside?"

"The relay panels. But it's kept locked. The key's with the desk clerk downstairs."

The lieutenant peered at the keyhole. "He should get this

one changed."

"Pardon me?"

He spoke to Purcelle. "It's been opened recently, these scratches are new."

Hocht took out a credit card, eased the blade of his penknife inside the keyhole and slid the plastic into the crack. After a moment or two, the door swung open and the sergeant looked up from his watch. "Fifteen seconds. Pretty slow, Gary." The lieutenant ignored him and stared at the panel.

"These relays . . . what happens if you change them over?"

The girl was pale. "I'm supposed to be responsible for the agency girls all the time they're here. I could lose my job!"

"We'll explain to Security before we leave," Hocht soothed. "Just show me."

When she'd finished this time, the sergeant commented, "Didn't look difficult and it was well inside three minutes."

"Did Miss Beeker need any more water?" asked Hocht, shutting the cupboard. The girl shook her head.

"I took an early break. She had twenty minutes all to herself while I grabbed a burger."

"Thanks."

Sammy scuffed his way along a Boulder City sidewalk. It had been going so well until his luck ran out. Charlene had been pleased, her eyes had shone making them an even deeper blue. Then he lost six times in a row, even the stake money had gone.

The others had been mad as hell, they'd driven off taking Charlene with them, leaving him stranded. Now all he could think of was how late it was, nearly 2.00 a.m.! Grandma would scold. Hell, it wasn't his fault; life was so unfair sometimes. Sammy stopped. Dead ahead, parked beyond the fire hydrant was the old pick-up. There was a note under the wiper blade in his grandmother's handwriting.

"To whom it may concern . . ." she had this funny English way of putting things. "Battery is flat. Garage will tow away tomorrow." Sammy became excited. There was nothing wrong with the battery but there was a loose connection his grandma didn't know about. With luck he might get home after all. But if she'd been hammering the ignition he'd need the crank. He began rummaging in the back.

A group of people had gathered in the roadway. Sammy could hear other English voices. Passers-by were standing to watch them argue. It looked like a movie crew but the cameraman sounded American.

"We know what Enrico wants. The two of you coming round that corner, going left to right past camera and out of shot. We pick you up *entering* the casino the following morning."

The young actor was sullen. "It's not my habit to work without a director."

"Over here, it happens *all* the time, especially when the shot isn't that important," the cameraman retorted. He pulled out his light-meter. Jed Pointer stalked off to where he'd been bidden.

Sammy found the crank. It wasn't anyone exciting like Harrison Ford, he might as well go home.

When John Millar entered the camper, still in his patrolman's uniform, his nerves were screwed to sticking point. The first thing he looked at was the television, still whispering away in the corner. Ozal was where he'd left him, at the desk. John experienced a fear he thought he'd conquered years ago; had Ozal heard the broadcast? If he hadn't, how was John going to prevent it next time? Those bulletins went out on the hour, every hour.

"John?"

"Hi." He had to know. "Everything OK?"

"Why did you do it?" There was a longish pause but John refused to reply, he couldn't. What was the use?

"OK," Ozal said quietly, "let's examine the situation. First, get it into your head you need me more than I shall ever need you. If you hadn't realised already, let me tell you now so you don't try anything else. You don't know all of the plan. I never tell anyone that. Call it . . . safety reasons. As for Judy Beeker, the Family knew we were using her. One of *them* heard the news and called me."

The blind eyes were staring right through him.

"And you think you're smart," Ozal leaned forward suddenly, his anger filling the space between. "Judy Beeker wouldn't have talked because she wanted her son back. You're so dumb you couldn't even work that out!"

No one called him dumb! Deep inside, hate crystallised, conquering fear. The Family would be watching him from now on, so what? They weren't omnipotent. He would obey Ozal's orders but as soon as this thing was over, he would kill him.

"I'm due back on duty," he muttered.

"So go. One wrong move from now on and you're dead." But it was an empty threat for the present, they both knew that; he still had his part to play, no one else could fly the helicopter. And when that was done? John calculated his reprieve at just under twenty-four hours.

Gino and his team had come into the desert from opposite directions. The two cars alongside one another, engines running, headlights dipped. Even though it was dark, the sickle scar was in place above his eyebrow. If he had to get out of the car, the coin was in his shoe to remind him to limp. The team leader knew what he looked like, they'd worked together in the past, but the secretive side of Gino's nature meant he wanted any casual labour to know him only as Jay Kuminsky.

"All set?" he asked.

"Sure. Checked and double-checked."

"OK, now the details."

He could feel them staring. Apart from the leader, these men had had a third of their money, now they all wanted to be told where the final pay-out was to be made.

"It's a farm building behind a ranch," Gino said, "an old barn." He repeated the address adding, "You go there in a stationery supplies truck. That will be here, tucked out of sight behind that band of scrub at around 2.00 a.m. – got that?"

They didn't reply, all eyes were fixed on him absorbing every detail.

"Use this to cover the other vehicle, make sure it's as well hidden as possible." Gino passed the pack of camouflage netting across. To the man who got out to put it in the truck he said, "The helicopters will be out searching by then."

"Sure."

"The track to the barn is pretty rough. The door will be locked, here's the key." This too was handed over. "The money will be in cartons. There's a mixture of packing cases already there." He and John had brought those in the helicopter on the first visit, to allay Shirley and Sammy's suspicions, but this he didn't bother to explain.

"The ones you're interested in will be the two grey boxes. Don't try and be cute and take any others . . . some of them only have paper inside like it says on the labels and you haven't got time to start looking.

"There's a woman and her grandson living on the property. The boy's not too bright but watch out for her. We don't want her identifying anyone after – and don't scare her, neither. All nice and business-like. If she asks, you're delivering paper to a new warehouse in Sante Fé."

"You'll be there?" asked one. Gino shook his head. He would be on the helicopter delivery flight with John but there was no need to tell them about that.

"You'll turn up like a normal collection and delivery service. Just the two, right?"

"Right," the leader agreed, "the others go back to work, like any other Monday. Two of us collect. When does the money get there? How soon after the heist?"

"That's none of your business, Al," Gino said evenly. "What you're to do is arrive around 9.00 a.m., not before. That's from the boss man himself, OK?" Ozal's orders had been specific.

In the darkness, one man hissed, "No double-cross, Kuminsky."

"No point. You could finger me any time you wanted to."

The three hired hands had worked that out, or believed they had. The leader winked. Gino ignored it. He wasn't planning to cheat; they'd done what he'd asked. "Same applies to me as it does to you," he went on, "I'm not planning on writing any memoirs, I'm relying on you to do the same." There was silence. "Any questions?" What they had to do was complicated but he'd been through it often enough. "OK, that's it. Have a good trip."

The two cars separated, one heading back to Vegas, the other into the desert.

It had all gone so terribly wrong. Louis wanted to yell. All because of that damn pooch! He thumped the steering wheel, frustrated tears pouring down. He was a small-time guy from New York, he should never have gotten mixed up in all this! God, what was he going to do now?

Without a coherent thought, he headed north and west away from the ranch. He had to lose these two, dump them for the next

68

twenty-four hours where they couldn't interfere. Never mind the plan, he'd think of yet another excuse to tell Ozal.

A sign flashed up out of the darkness. Automatically, he took the left fork, heading further west, skirting Las Vegas and on towards the California border. This destination would mean driving through the night in order to be back at Boulder City by morning. He had no choice. He had to lose them where they wouldn't be picked up in a hurry and then drive like hell to get back to the filming.

"I didn't want it to be like this," he moaned. He should've killed them; John or Ozal would've done so, maybe even Gino. Nor should he have left the old woman alive. She might bleed to death. Hell, if she didn't, if the crazy grandson found her in time, she might find some way to call the police even though he'd cut the phone. If she did, the Family would know who to blame!

Oh God . . . Louis had never been in such a spot: so much for using his charm to make her do things his way. He was up against his own weak nature, there was no one else to blame. After the business with the dog, he couldn't think straight. He'd shot at it – and missed. The pooch whimpered when he saw the knife. *He* knew what Louis was about to do, right up to the end. And then he'd panicked and shot the woman but he'd only managed to wound her – at a range of ten feet!

Louis was crying openly now. Beth was so right, he was out of his league. If killing a dog was too much, how could he handle anything bigger?

God Almighty, why did those two have to turn up? Out of the whole of America how did they come to be at that ranch? Who had told them about it?

He'd shouted questions at them after he'd stuffed gags in their mouths. He'd been a real shithead tonight!

Louis's brain still couldn't accept what had happened. That two interfering idiots could turn his existence into a nightmare. Why hadn't remembered how sentimental the Brits were over animals? It was only a dog, for Chrissake, why'd she have to attack him like that?

"How the hell did you know where to come, though?" he yelled again.

His question went unanswered by the helpless bodies, one of them unconscious, both bound and gagged in the trunk.

Chapter Five

Dawn on the 17th

Mr Pringle had never felt so ill. As he regained consciousness, early sunlight, harsh and unrelenting, blinded him. Above his head was a broken window-pane. Below that, dangling from a wallbracket, a smashed wash-basin. His head was cushioned on rubble. As far as he could make out he was in a small, empty room with dingy blue plaster walls.

The gag had gone but his arms were still tied behind his back. At first they'd been lifeless; now, as sensation began to return, the pain was excruciating. The bonds were tight, leaving his hands nothing but useless lumps of swollen hot flesh.

His legs hadn't been bound quite so fiercely. Mr Pringle experimented by flexing a knee but the movement jerked his bound arms. He screamed and in a corner of the room, another bundle stirred and groaned. He could have wept for joy; Mrs Bignell was with him and obviously alive.

"Where am I . . . What's going on?" she muttered thickly.

"Mavis? Can you hear me?"

"Of course I can. Where are we?"

He looked around. "It appears to be an empty bungalow."

Mrs Bignell rolled over on to her side. "Oh, my God," she whimpered, "my arms don't half hurt!"

"So do mine. Can you move your legs?" A familiar, plump foot lifted six inches off the floor and the toes began to waggle. "Can you sit up?" She tried but the agony was too much.

"No I bloody can't!" She was crying and he desperately wanted to comfort her.

"Cheer up. At least he didn't kill us."

She was bewildered. "What happened to the man? Did he have a brainstorm?"

"I've no idea." Various thoughts had been churning away but so far none of them made sense.

"It's my fault we're here," she moaned. "You didn't want to come to America in the first place."

"No," he admitted. "As holidays go, this one hasn't been without incident however. It may improve," he added valiantly but she wouldn't be consoled.

"You haven't got a home to go back to, either. That oven's bound to have blown up by now."

"What I can't understand is how Dulce came to be there and why he should behave with such extraordinary unprovoked violence."

"That poor dog – "

"Don't!" When he'd recovered, Mr Pringle asked, "Did you hear what he was saying, before he pushed you over?"

"He was shouting so much I couldn't make out any of it."

"I've never seen a man so deranged. You and I seemed to act as some sort of trigger, though I'm blessed if I can fathom why. As soon as he saw us, Dulce began to bellow that it had all gone wrong, that it was my fault, then he pointed to that unfortunate animal and said he owed it to Beth. Who's Beth?"

"God knows," she replied. "I thought we were going to suffocate in that car boot." Tears began once more. "Something must've snapped to make Enrico behave like that. He's been so nice up to now."

"But how on earth did he come to be at Shirley's ranch, behaving like a burglar? The place is in the middle of nowhere – "

"Shirley!" The sobbing ceased abruptly. "What happened to her, d'you remember?" Mr Pringle recalled only too vividly.

"After you'd taken a swing at Dulce with your handbag – I think you'd overlooked the fact that he had a gun – "

"I didn't care," she said simply. "I was so *angry* when I saw that dog, I didn't stop to think. Anyway, they all have guns out here. I can't think why. I haven't seen a single Indian since we arrived, have you? Oh, I shall be glad to get home." So would Mr Pringle but he tried not to think of the difficulties that lay between them and their objective.

"After you hit him, Dulce punched you; you fell over and knocked your head against the table. I'm afraid he then fired his gun at Shirley."

"Whatever for? He didn't kill her!"

"I don't think so. She went very quiet, but she was bleeding from her shoulder. That's supposed to be a good sign, isn't it?"

"Fantastic," said Mavis flatly. "All you want when you come home after a good night out. What were you doing all this while?"

"Being sick," he admitted. "I tried to avoid the rug. As Dulce was tying me up I did point out that he was being extremely unwise. Unfortunately he stuffed a tea-cloth in my mouth. I couldn't think rationally after that, I was so terrified of choking. He must have removed it before he left us here." One memory shamed him. "I fear I made no pugilistic effort to defend you, for which I apologise. It wasn't out of lack of affection, Mavis."

"Thank goodness you didn't. After what he did to that dog, I hate to think what might have happened." As she shifted slightly, Mrs Bignell made an unfortunate discovery. "Blast! It must've been when we were in that boot – I'll never forgive him – I've wet my knickers."

"It couldn't be helped," Mr Pringle said tenderly.

"It's the last straw," she announced, furious. "And why bring us here where it's so bloomin' hot? Now the sun's getting up, it's right in my eyes. I'm parched, all that wine last night, I expect. Oh, God, how long before we're rescued?"

He tried to divert her. "Can you see anything?" After a painful struggle, Mavis swivelled round far enough to gaze through an empty window-frame.

"We're on the ground floor . . . You're right, it is a single storey because I can see a bit of roof . . . and a white column. Stucco. Like those 1930 bungalows on the Great West Road. It looks derelict. Here, you don't think we've been abandoned?"

"No . . . " He was faint from the pain in his limbs, "John Wayne's bound to come riding into the town at sunset, you said so yourself."

"He's dead," Mavis said sadly, "like Bing Crosby." There was no response. "Wake up," then, more loudly, "don't go to sleep, it's bad for you in your condition." But Mr Pringle ignored her for once and floated off into blessed unconsciousness.

Outside the casino in Boulder City, Monica Moffat had finished her arrival scenes with Ivor Henry. She sat watching as Enrico

72

Dulce directed the remaining shots with Jed and Clarissa.

He'd offered no explanation for his absence the previous evening; this morning he was red-eyed as if from lack of sleep. There was no time wasted coaxing a performance out of Jed. Instead, when the actor resorted to the old trick of swearing to ensure a shot be retaken, Dulce called to the crew, "Next position, camera at the top of the casino steps."

"You're never going to use that?" Jed was incredulous but Dulce ignored him.

Beside her, Ivor Henry said viciously, "That'll teach our young friend not to be so unprofessional."

"Maybe," Monica was unconvinced. "I agree with Jed, though; I don't quite see how they can edit it out, do you?"

"It's not our problem, sweety."

"Enrico's very tense. He never stops looking at his watch."

"I've every sympathy. It's a tight schedule and Jed knows it. He shouldn't make mistakes. Hallo, here come the traffic cops. Where's Pringle? He should be smoothing the path and arranging the permissions, not the director. No wonder Enrico's looking tired."

They watched as Dulce expostulated, obviously begging for more time. They heard the familiar argument begin, that filming was causing crowds to build up on the pavement.

"Only ten more minutes, I swear," Dulce was saying. "We have to leave for Vegas, we're due to film there this evening."

The police gave grudging consent and Dulce strode over to where Monica was sitting. "Sweetheart, could you order iced coffee for all of us, including the cops?"

"Shall I find Pringle for you?" offered Ivor. "He could make himself useful for once. He should be here anyway."

"Pringle's in Vegas," Louis assured him blandly. "There wasn't much to do here, he's gone ahead to check the rooms, fix the locations, etc. OK, everyone, let's get started on the next shot. It's Jed and Clarissa going up the steps and into the casino."

Monica watched his retreating back. "That's odd. I didn't see them leave."

Ivor shrugged. "They must have gone while you were still asleep."

"Maybe. Iced coffee for how many?"

"About fifteen, at a guess. It's a small enough crew, God

knows, and I'm never sure whether make-up or wardrobe want to be included. They're a very secretive lot, aren't they? Not ones for socialising."

"No . . . " Monica's gaze was still on Dulce. "I think you and I ought to get changed for our next scene. Enrico seems so edgy, we don't want to keep him waiting."

It had taken Sammy a long time to get the pick-up started, then half-way home he'd run out of gas. He'd hitched a lift but had to wait until the garage owner arrived to open up. The man let him have a gallon but he'd had to walk back to the pick-up. No vehicles had passed.

He was rubbing his eyes to fight off sleep as he drove down the track to the ranch, rehearsing excuses for his grandma.

He slowed at the point where Bomber usually came to meet him, then he saw it, parked in front of the verandah: a shiny new car with its lights still on. A real beamer of a car! Hey, who'd leave a thing like that out here? Maybe Mr Kuminsky had come calling again with more dollars? Sammy pulled up eagerly beside it.

"It's me, I'm back," he shouted. Through the mesh he could see the light on inside the kitchen. "Grandma? Mr Kuminsky?" He stepped over the threshold and heard the flies before he understood why there were so many. "Bomber . . . " It was a croak. Shock thumped the breath out of him. "Bomber!" It was a howl. He was on his knees beside the mess, reaching out to touch stiff, dead fur.

From inside the closet in his room, Shirley used all her strength to push against the door. The flimsy latch finally gave way and her trussed, blood-stained body rolled over on to the floor. Sammy appeared and rushed across, yanking his knife from his belt.

"Grandma, Grandma – what's happened to you? They've killed Bomber, Grandma. They've cut his throat . . . they've killed my Bomber!"

Shirley had lost so much blood he was nothing but a blur. She'd spent the last hour wondering if she'd die before he got back. As soon as he'd cut the scarf from round her mouth, she gasped, "Listen, Sammy, be quiet and listen to what I say. There was a gunman here when we got back last night, he killed

Bomber. Two Brits gave me a lift home. He shot me through the shoulder then he tied them up and took them with him." Sammy's slow wits tried to keep up.

"You mean, Mr Kuminsky did it? He was waiting for you?"

"Oh, bloody hell!" Shirley was trying to flex livid, painful fingers. The police could be told later, provided she survived. She concentrated on the essentials. "You've got to get me to a doctor, Sammy."

"It must've been Mr Freeman, Grandma. Mr Kuminsky's kind. He wouldn't have done that to Bomber."

Neither was the name Mavis had used. Shirley was too ill to think clearly; one conviction remained, that Mavis and Mr Pringle had recognised the bastard. She wondered for the umpteenth time whether they were all in some kind of conspiracy.

"Blood . . . blood all down your dress, Grandma," whimpered Sammy. Biting her lip, she eased the pad that her assailant had tied round the wound.

"Get me a clean towel from the bathroom shelf." When he came running back, she asked, "Did you find the pick-up?"

"Yes, but it's nearly out of gas."

"You have to get me to a doctor right away," she cried desperately.

"There's a big new car outside."

The hire car she realised thankfully.

"We'll use that. You'll have to drive. Go carefully now. Take me to Casualty. Never mind if I pass out, you just keep on driving. Don't talk to anyone. Don't stop till you get to the hospital, promise me now."

"Yes, Grandma."

"Help me."

He half-carried her past Bomber and down the steps. The heat sapped her remaining strength, she could barely stay upright in the seat.

"Fill a bottle of water." She needed to stay alive. Sammy, anxious to make amends, returned with a six-pack of Coke.

"It's good for you, Grandma. It says so on TV."

"Get started. Hurry now." Each pothole made her wince. They should go to the police as soon as they got to Boulder but Sammy was implicated up to the neck. When they had given her something for the pain and she could think straight, that's when she would decide.

"You all right, Grandma?"

"Just you keep driving," she whispered.

As if reading her thoughts, he said, "Mr Freeman said they'd kill me if I told anyone. Why did they have to do that to Bomber? He was a good dog, he never hurt anyone." He began to whimper again, "Grandma, I'm scared!"

Someone had phoned the department following the news item on TV. When Sergeant Purcelle and Lieutenant Hocht returned, they were given the message. "Seems Mrs Beeker visited the dry cleaners last week," the lieutenant told Purcelle, dialling the number, "the manageress wants to tell us about it." He listened as a woman's voice answered then introduced himself. The sergeant picked up the extension.

The manageress was garrulous and wandered from the point. When she paused, Hocht asked politely, "Did Mrs Beeker discuss anything during her visit?"

The woman remembered why she'd phoned.

"She was checking the pockets of a skirt, see. There was a photo of her kid. As soon as she saw it, she said she might be seeing him again real soon. It was important, I could tell. Mrs Beeker was smiling. You know, happy."

"Did she say *when* she might be seeing him?"

"Just . . . soon."

"Or where?"

"No. Although . . . "

"Yes?"

"Sounded as if *he* would be coming to *her* rather than the other way round. She never said where Scott was, though. I don't reckon she knew."

"Anything else?"

"She collected a jacket for someone."

"Well, thanks anyway." As he hung up, Hocht said briskly, "Maybe we should concentrate on Scott Beeker. Have we any details yet?"

Purcelle began leafing through papers on the desk. "We need to know who paid the bail bond when he disappeared."

"Sure."

The phone rang and Hocht picked it up. "Homicide . . . Yes? That's interesting, thanks." This time he said, "I think we may have a break. That drawer he put her in, remember the tight fit, how she was practically folded in half? He had to force her body down real hard and the fluids were already beginning to escape. He used a face-cloth to clean up. It's just been found, wedged under the lid of the toilet tank."

"Careless," commented Purcelle, surprised.

"With luck there'll be traces on him, too. He'll have changed his clothes, but he may not have put the old ones in the washing machine."

It was an old truck, decorated with luridly depicted scenes of eternal damnation. On one panel, the stern injunction, LOVE GOD; on another, BEWARE THE GODDESS WHORE, with a bosomy strawberry blonde, ill-clad for chariot racing, whipping up her horses.

The driver was morose, full of thoughts of present discomfort rather than salvation. His vehicle rattled past clumps of desert holly and cactus but he no longer noticed, it was so goddamn hot.

There were dust devils skimming across the macadam, grit was in his skin and eyes and he knew he needed to check the radiator before he ventured too far into the Valley. He'd had to change a tire in Tecopa. Maybe Big Joe would agree a trade-in? He'd stop there anyway, at the junction. Pause awhile. Hell, a man didn't have to kill himself in the service of the Lord.

There were mountains stretching from earth to heaven reaching to a limitless sky. He could use them next time he preached the Word. What the fuck were those hills called? No matter. They were volcanic, he remembered that much. Volcanic with patches of sand. The devil's dwelling place – Hell!

Wisps of steam were rising from the bonnet.

"Get me there, baby. You can do it. Not far now," he crooned. The end of the world was nigh, no doubt about it, what with the Arabs and Israelis threatening to nuke one another, but as usual his prayer was for the old truck to last a little longer. As Enoch's prophet, among the hierachy of the Chosen, God would surely show recognition with a Chevvie, but for the present, "Keep going, baby" the prophet begged. The bend was ahead now. Beyond was the derelict hotel. God, he needed a slash! The prophet put a little more pressure on the gas.

Inside the filthy room, Mavis Bignell was extremely worried. She didn't know how long they'd been there but judging by the position of the sun, several hours.

It was no longer burning her skin but the heat was still intense. With the slight drop in temperature, came another torment. She'd been bitten. They had bigger bugs in America than any she'd seen before, even at Weston-super-Mare. Worst of all, she couldn't get a peep out of the body under the wash-basin.

She'd called his name several times. She'd tried scolding, everything. Once, she thought she heard a sound. Eventually she was too exhausted to try any more. She could do nothing but pant, her mouth was so dry, even her lips were cracked.

Dust wafted down as the wind increased. Mrs Bignell had a panicky moment when she wondered if they'd be smothered to death. She listened for breathing from the opposite corner. By twisting her body, she could glimpse Mr Pringle's face. It was a nasty colour; her heart turned over at the thought she might lose him. Out here, of all places. In this disgusting, dirty . . . Hallo? What was that?

Vehicles had gone past before. This building must be on some kind of S-bend because engines changed up and down through the gears. This time though, the noise belonged to something slow and tired. Glory be, it was stopping!

Mavis tried to shout. She could hear footsteps, or thought she could. The wind made unseen trees creak and this blotted out other sounds.

She was straining to catch those footsteps again. "Hey!" It was a whisper, she'd have to manage better than that. A noise reached her. Whoever it was, was whistling! Mavis gathered herself for a final effort when something most unpleasant happened.

Warm yellow liquid began spilling over the sill and trickling down the wall beside her ear. The sight restored her inner strength.

"Hey!" cried Mrs Bignell. "Stop that at once!"

"Jesus!" said the prophet of Enoch, "Jesus Christ!"

"Mavis Bignell, actually, but before we go any further, would you kindly put that away."

"Aw, shit . . . Sorry, ma'am . . . Sor-ree!" He jiggled with his zip. As she couldn't avert her gaze, Mrs Bignell lowered her lids.

"Have you a knife or a pair of scissors?"

"Pardon me?"

"We've been tied up. My friend's in a bad way. Be as quick as you can."

A leather-heeled boot hovered in front of her face and reached the floor. Both legs were clad in the inevitable jeans, the body in a fringed suede jacket, but it was the hat which fascinated her. An ancient shiny leather stetson, it had feathers stuck into the band and a fur tail dangling down the back.

The man took a knife from a sheath on his leg. He was an unshaven, grubby cowboy. John Wayne he certainly wasn't but under the circumstances, she wasn't going to complain.

"Free my friend first, please," she insisted. "I'm afraid he's very poorly."

The prophet of Enoch took one look at Mr Pringle and said, high-pitched, "He sure looks dead to me."

"He will be if you don't hurry up."

"Sorry, ma'am." The blade moved rapidly.

"And do be careful with that thing, you might nick a vein. Can you do first aid?"

"Pardon me?"

She sighed. There was no doubt about it, theirs was not a common language.

"When you've cut him free, do you think you could find a glass of water?" she asked, slowly and distinctly. "Mr Pringle is dehydrated, as am I." The knife sliced through her own bonds. An enormous wave of pain surged through her arms and shoulders.

"Oh! Oh, my Lord!" Mrs Bignell gasped for air – she'd never known such agony – "I think I'm going to be sick!"

"Hang on," begged the cowboy, "I'll fetch Big Joe. He'll know what to do."

For a few moments she concentrated on staying alive, fighting the pain that threatened her whole being, then blessed cold water suddenly sloshed over her face and neck. Mrs Bignell opened her eyes. A small, elderly hippy was emptying the rest of the bucket over Mr Pringle. From the back she could see his pants were held together with patches, he wore a dirty tie-dye shirt and a headband held elfin locks in position around a bald pate. It was a gnome on a rescue mission.

There was a cough from Mr Pringle followed by a splutter. "He's alive!" The gnome was obviously amazed. Ignoring protests from her body, Mrs Bignell crawled across through the dirt.

"Hallo, dear," she said loudly. "Wake up. It's all right, we've been rescued." She turned to the hippy, "Did I hear your name correctly?"

"Yes, ma'am. Big Joe."

When Mr Pringle regained consciousness it was to find an anxious group staring down. Closest to him was Mavis, who sighed with relief.

"Thank God for that."

"Where are we . . ?" he asked faintly.

"In Death Valley, dear. This is Joseph and that's the prophet of Enoch, who's also known as Irwin."

Perhaps it had been presumption to imagine himself destined for Paradise but as long as Mrs Bignell was with him, Mr Pringle was content.

"Can you sit up?" Pain returned with a vengeance, bringing with it the realisation he was still attached to the planet.

"Oh! Oh, dear me!"

"Yes, I know," she said patiently. "It's ghastly, isn't it? Makes you want to cry like a baby. Don't worry about us, let yourself go." And to divert attention from his distress, she asked, "Which of you two owns the lorry?"

"D'you mean my old truck, ma'am?" said Irwin. "I'd stopped by to do a bit of business with Big Joe here."

"Well, I'm sorry but you'll have to leave that till some other time. We were mugged by a burglar at a ranch last night. He tied us up and brought us here, but – and this is what makes it so important – he shot the lady who owns the ranch in the shoulder. We have to find her as quickly as possible and get her to a doctor."

The man of God revealed his limitations.

"You mean, he had a gun? I don't see how there's any necessity to go looking for trouble – "

"It's all right," Mavis assured him, "Mr Pringle and I know him. He's the reason we're in America, as a matter of fact, and I'm sure he was only having a brainstorm because of what he'd done to the dog. He'd tried to cut the poor thing's head off, you see. There was a shocking mess but don't you worry about that. When we find the ranch, Mr Pringle and I will have a little chat and persuade Mr Dulce to give himself up while you two take Shirley to the nearest hospital."

Big Joe and Irwin were dumbfounded.

"Go and talk to a maniac? You mad, lady?" Big Joe squeaked rather than spoke.

"We can't leave Shirley to bleed to death, can we?" Mavis demanded tartly. "Now, show me this vehicle of yours."

She was determined Mr Pringle should travel as comfortably as possible. When they were out of earshot, she explained, "My friend also needs to see a doctor but I don't want him to know how worried I am. As soon as we've collected Shirley we'll take both of them to the Casualty department – Oh my Lord, where has he brought us to?"

Big Joe puffed out his diminutive chest.

"Well ma'am, that's the Valley you're looking at. Down in that direction is Furnace Creek and over there, those are the Funeral Mountains."

Mavis stared at a towering range twice as high as anything she'd seen before.

"You travel the other way, you'll find Coffin Canyon and the Devil's Golf Course. Down the road there . . . " He pointed with pride, "it's almost three hundred feet below sea-level. It gets so hot, birds have to lie on their backs to let their feet cool off."

Mrs Bignell gazed about in consternation: it was like being in the Sahara. She was in an enormous desert, that was obvious. There was no sign of a town. As far as the eye could see, the road headed through scrub towards a bare white plain with more mountains beyond. A cruel sun shimmered on distant white Borax workings, making her blink. Whichever way she looked, there wasn't another living soul.

The white stucco building was a derelict hotel with a colonnade fronting on to a dusty square with trees. Beyond these was the bend in the road. Opposite was a ramshackle collection of huts, telegraph posts and a water-tower. To her left, at right angles to the colonnade, a smartly painted entrance with a fire-hose outside had a sign that left her flabbergasted.

"Amargosa Opera House!"

"Sure thing," Big Joe squeaked proudly. "Lady who owns it is a fine artist and dancer. She's been on TV, you know. What you're looking at over there," he indicated the collection of huts across the road, "is our transportation business." He shook his head over the rusting wrecks. "People die in Death Valley. Doesn't matter how often you tell 'em – if their car breaks down and they try and walk to safety – they die. Happens every time."

She was in a cultural oasis-cum-garage at the end of the world; her mouth felt as parched as the desert floor.

"But where's Boulder City," Mavis demanded. "How far did Enrico bring us, for heaven's sake?"

"Boulder City? Hell, lady, now you're talking big distance." The prophet of Enoch looked mutinous. "My ol' truck ain't going on that kinda trip, not with the radiator leaking all the time."

But Big Joe was eager for a break in routine.

"Lady doesn't want *us* to meet up with the guy, Irwin. We could take her as far as that; I'll bring my tools, we can keep the truck going. You could pitch your tent in Boulder, do a spot of preaching."

"Oh yes, there are plenty of sinners in Boulder City," Mavis said confidently, "not like here." She gazed at the lorry with its messages of hope and damnation. It was a pity about John Wayne but in an emergency one couldn't be fussy. "If you plan holding an open-air service, Irwin, perhaps Mr Pringle and I could take the plate round afterwards," she suggested cordially. "Any chance of a wash before we go?"

Big Joe led her through a clump of trees, startling a pair of road runners, and revealed a large muddy pond; it was an oasis after all. "Help yourself, lady," he said munificently, "no charge for using the facilities at Death Valley Junction."

It was an odd rescue party that set forth twenty minutes later. Mr Pringle had been revived and cushioned by a sleeping bag on one side, and Mrs Bignell's magnificent flank on the other. Despite his poor state, as that warm luscious thigh rubbed against his own, Mr Pringle knew again that life was worth living. He wanted to tell her so. As she fastened the seat-belt across his sore ribs, he gave her hand a little squeeze: it was sufficient, Mrs Bignell wrinkled her nose in a gesture he understood.

Squashed at the end of the row, Big Joe had changed out of the filthy headband into a bright yellow bandana, in honour of the expedition. Hugging the wheel, convinced it was all a mistake, the prophet of Enoch stared sulkily through the windscreen. Mavis tried to improve his temper.

"Tell me about this religion of yours," she invited. "Is Enoch one of the books in the Old Testament? I don't think I remember it at Sunday School?" It was a starting pistol: Irwin was away from the blocks in a thousandth of a second.

"Why no, ma'am. There's the book of Revelations, of course. We're keen on that. Us followers of Enoch think very highly of the Bible, particularly the book of Daniel. But Enoch is more than all of these put together. He's the One, oh, boy, is he the One! He's prophesied the end of the world, and do you know why? Because of your European Common Market." Mavis realised she'd made a mistake.

"Fancy." But there was a gleam in the prophet's eye which could not be quenched; how long since anyone had *invited* him to preach the Word?

"Enoch has been foretelling the future ever since May 16 1973," he cried with increasing fervour. "He sure cocked a snook at Nostradamus and those old phonies. Enoch has given us his solemn word that when the Goddess whore comes forth from the Common Market, driving her red chariot, we sure better look out!"

"Does he mean Mrs Thatcher?" murmured Mavis. Mr Pringle shifted uneasily.

"He may be using a metaphor."

"Inside that chariot will be the man with the mark on his forehead and the withered right arm. He will be slain by the Evil One but lo – thanks to the bio-chip in his forehead – he will rise up and conquer the World!"

"So Mrs Thatcher will only be a sort of taxi driver?" It was a sliver of comfort. Big Joe nudged Mavis as near to her ribs as he could reach.

"Irwin's a mighty fine preacher," he said admiringly. "He can talk like that for hours," but she had heard enough.

"What about a hymn? I do enjoy a sing-song. Come on, altogether, after four . . . "

Along the road to Baker the old truck rumbled. Within, a quavering soprano led an uncertain tenor and a squeaker in a kind of unison:

> "Like a mighty ar-ar-army,
> Moves the church of God.
> Brothers we are treading,
> Where the saints have trod . . . pom-di-pom."

Aching all over, Mr Pringle wondered whether, even with the additional forces they'd gathered under their banner, he and Mrs Bignell dare risk confronting an armed Enrico Dulce.

> "Forward into ba-a-ttle,
> See his banners go,
> Ba-ba-bom, ba-ba-bom, ba-ba-bom . . . "

His head throbbed, every muscle protested at having been deprived of a blood supply for so long. Worse, thoughts which had been churning away suddenly began to make sense. He turned a deaf ear to the singing as a pattern began to emerge. The trouble was, if true – and his bowels turned to water at the very possibility – what was his next step? Dare he take it?

> "Onward Christian so-o-oldiers,
> Marching as to wa-ar!
> With the cross of Jesus,
> Going on be-fore!"

Chapter Six

The top bank of screens showed shots of the Star's stand-in as the director talked quietly into his mike. Like everyone else, he was pacing himself for what would be a long transmission. In the control room the rest of the team went about their business, counting on air, intercutting pictures, standing-by the overseas links.

"Camera three slaved to Frank throughout."

"Check."

"Two, I want you to stay wide at the start of each new act. We don't know how much of the stage some of them are going to use." Camera two tilted in acknowledgement.

"How's the crane doing?"

The switcher punched up the outside overhead shot.

"Nice," the director murmured appreciatively. "Show me on the zoom." A group of faces among the crowds on the sidewalk came into sharp focus. "Great . . . smooth. Find me a better looking chick and we'll use that. How's the link with Rome?"

"Still having trouble with the sound."

"Keep trying. If some Italian fan wants to donate a million lira, we need to hear her do it."

"Five minutes . . . five minutes!"

"OK, let's rehearse the opening shots following the VT. Everyone else go back to the top. We'll take the crane shot – I like that brunette, stay with her. Zoom in tight when I give the word; second thoughts, stay in mid shot, she's got great boobs. Go from that to the helicopter arriving. Who's available by the landing pad?"

"Gene. Right here, Joe."

"OK. Walk it through for me, will you. I want to see Mr

Sinatra on the hand-held as soon as the door opens . . . and cue."

"Coming out of titles in five . . . four . . . "

On the pavement outside the Beaux Rêves, Mrs Ellis and her family had made themselves comfortable with sleeping bags and camping stools. Her daughter-in-law produced iced drinks and Mrs Ellis looked at her watch. "D'you think he'll be on time? The royal family always are, they're famous for it."

In the Homicide department, TVs were on in every office, including the captain's, but those gathered for the case conference pretended to ignore it. Lieutenant Gary Hocht tried to hold his boss's attention.

"What we've been able to confirm adds up to very little but it indicates a particular direction. According to Scott Beeker's file, his mother stood bail – and paid cash when he disappeared." Eyebrows went up opposite. "As far as we've been able to check, she never had anything like that amount in her account at the time."

"She have a boyfriend?" asked the captain. This time Rob Purcelle replied.

"I've only had time to speak to one former neighbour but he can't recall anybody. After her husband died, Mrs Beeker devoted herself to Scott but there wasn't enough insurance money so she had to go back to full-time work. That's when Scott began to pick up bad habits. Got a wild reputation. Took after his father, everyone said. He began peddling drugs but was never caught."

"So an involvement going back some time?"

"That's the way we see it. We hope to confirm it when we talk to Mrs Beeker's sister in Little Rock. If it was a gang supplying him it might account for the bail money."

The captain sighed. "No leads?"

"None."

Lieutenant Hocht fidgeted. "This blind guy . . . ?"

"Yes, lieutenant?"

"We tried a man of a similar build on the old lady. She came up with a few extra pointers, like he was wearing light-coloured clothing, things like that. We haven't found anything on file. I was thinking, though . . . "

"Yes?"

"He has this companion. She thought it looked as if he was *needing* a guide. Seemed to me, behaving like that, he could have gone blind late in life." The captain considered.

"Not used to it yet?" That wasn't quite what Hocht meant.

"More that he hadn't *accepted* the blindness if he was still wanting a buddy. The way the old lady described it, he knew which way to walk – wouldn't take much to find the right button in the elevator – so why the male guide dog?" There was a grunt.

"If they're a gang, they might need to work in pairs, you mean? Guesswork, Gary, pure guesswork. And where does that leave us?"

Not perturbed by this assessment, Hocht took the question as an invitation to stretch his legs.

"It has to be the appeal," he insisted stubbornly. "Even if we haven't worked out the connection, the timing is too coincidental."

The captain shrugged. "We know most of the regular bad boys in town. We even have details of how some were planning to do the snitch . . . " With deep satisfaction, he added, "Thank God that's not my responsibility. One dead operator is enough."

He broke off to watch the silenced TV; the appeal had finally begun. The Star having been secretly whisked back up from the ground, now descended out of the heavens by helicopter, for better effect. As shown by the hand-held camera he walked the length of the red carpet and ran lightly up the steps into the palatial mirrored entrance, arriving eventually at the dais.

Glittering on its plinth, the golden bowl was already piled with pledges made before the programme began. A ribbon of names was superimposed on the screen; among several large sponsors were the names of ordinary people whose moment of glory had finally come. Shots of the smiling Star were intercut with whooping soundless faces as onlookers yelled their appreciation.

"When that crazy idea first began . . . " drawled the captain, "of taking twenty-three million unmarked notes down the Strip at the finish to show everybody, I took a bet, not on how many millions they'd make – Frank Sinatra's capable of raising that much any Saturday – but on whether the money would ever reach the bank."

"What odds?" asked Purcelle, interested.

"Not good."

"In front of all those people?"

The captain pulled a face. "A couple of the best criminal brains in America began working on the problem as soon as the idea first hit the media. Thank God we know who *some* of them are. We can publish their mug shots tomorrow if we have to, to prove that we weren't sitting on our butts when the heist finally came.

"The only one that won't be up there – according to your theory, lieutenant – is the guy we don't know yet, who strangled Judy Beeker. She must've known him. A pity we don't have a spiritualist on the strength."

It was an old joke. The captain raised his hand at the sight of Hocht's protest, "I know you're doing your best but if that's all you've come up with, you've got a long way to go. I agree with you on one thing though, there are too many people in uniforms walking the streets right now."

"Sir, I would like to have all the names on the security passes rechecked."

"We've done that a thousand times already!"

"I realise but there could've been last-minute changes we don't know about. We had to delegate the issuing of late passes to the heads of the security firms themselves. They haven't got access to some of our records."

"Point taken. Anything else?"

"Yes, I want the best brains in *this* department to start asking our computer questions. Someone who knows about those psycho profiles we've been reading about. It could be that one of the bad boys has slipped through the net and is walking around town looking official." He didn't add: and carrying a gun. The captain understood. He tapped one of the files on the desk.

"The killer took all the usual precautions; he wore gloves. If he's goofed up in any way, which is unlikely, he may have traces of urine, blood, lipstick or even Beeker's skin particles on his clothing. He may be a blind sixty year old, or he may be all gussied up in his mid to late twenties. But . . . " he looked at both of them, "according to the autopsy, after he'd strangled Beeker, he hit her hard on the back of the skull. Any idea why he bothered to do that?"

Gary Hocht had attended the autopsy. "We were discussing it, it's one of the reasons I want a profile done. Beeker was dead by then, he must've known that. Before he killed her, she managed to yell. I wondered if the killer was punishing her in some way."

"Seems a mite over-thorough. Maybe you're right, though. A vicious bastard? If he spent time doing what was *unnecessary*, he's not as professional as we thought."

"He had no motive we've been able to discover," Hocht pointed out. "Nothing was taken. Her bits of jewellery and stuff were on the dressing table, there was money in her purse."

"So . . . You got *any* ideas at all?"

"I reckon we should concentrate on the internal call which must've been made during the period Judy Beeker switched relays."

"You're convinced that's what she did?"

Hocht shrugged. "It was only three minutes and there were scratches on the cupboard door. There ain't much else you can do in the communications room, it's kind of small."

"The Beaux Rêves isn't."

The lieutenant paused in his perambulations to gaze at the TV screen.

"We could certainly use some extra help. If it is to do with the appeal, it won't happen until all the money's in. I reckon we have a few more hours."

"Have a good day."

"Thanks," said Hocht.

In Boulder City, Monica Moffat shut out all thought of the curious people who'd paused to watch them work. It was a good part and she had reached the key line of her most crucial scene; she wanted to give of her best. She took her eyeline where Ivor Henry would have stood had he not been replaced by the camera, and waited.

"Rolling."

"Ident . . ."

"Shot 132 take one."

"In your own time," Louis said, automatically. Monica took a slow deep breath.

"'It's no use asking me to reconsider, not after all this time. What we had – it's gone, don't you understand?'" She waited as Ivor Henry fed her his cue from behind Enrico Dulce.

"'We can begin again, Laura. People do.'"

89

It was a tight shot; Monica's headshake was almost imperceptible.

"'It's gone,'" she repeated. "'What I have to do now is stop Jenny making the same mistake. I'll go anywhere . . . do anything.'" There was a catch in her voice as it dropped for the final words, "'I must!'" A car horn blared across the street.

"Blast!" said Louis, still engrossed in her performance. "Camera still rolling?"

"Affirmative."

"And again, sweetheart, from Ivor's line." Monica gave an identical tiny headshake, kept her gaze level and with the same catch in her throat, repeated the words, this time without interruption.

"And – cut." Louis went instinctively to kiss her on the cheek. "Terrific, sweetheart." The cameraman brought him back to the business in hand.

"It's one–thirty, Enrico."

"What? Oh, sure . . . OK, everyone, that's a wrap here. Get changed, grab a bite to eat and be out of your rooms by two-thirty. We leave for Vegas at three o'clock."

As the actors hurried off, it was the soundman who put the awkward question.

"Is the Pringle guy coming back, or what?"

They all knew it was part of Ozal's plan that the company manager should establish his presence in Las Vegas by arriving with the actors, then be seen abroad on the Strip. Louis's palms began to sweat.

"That's been changed – I sent Pringle ahead, there was a snarl-up over the first location," he improvised. "I darn well forgot to warn him to come back. Don't worry about it, the Brits can travel with me, it won't change anything."

But it wasn't what was supposed to happen. The cameraman asked pointedly, "You going to call Ozal and explain?"

Louis pretended to be deep in thought.

"Right now . . . no," he said decisively. "He's busy . . . very, very busy and it's not that important."

"We were supposed to establish the guy leaving here with the Brits," the cameraman insisted.

Louis forced himself to sound confident. "I know that. Hell, I'll talk to the desk clerk and mention Pringle good and loud."

He strode off, his mind fizzing. The waves were coming in faster and faster, if he could just keep his head above water till midnight . . .

It was lunchtime and Irwin's truck needed a rest. They had stopped at Baker, where the road from Death Valley joined the interstate highway. Impatient to be gone, Mavis left the crowded diner as soon as she'd finished, and sat outside. Mr Pringle joined her. They sheltered from the heat under a garage's red and white awning. Behind, brass animals on a roadside stall glittered in the hot dry air.

"You're not very talkative," she grumbled after a pause, "what's the matter? Are you feeling poorly again?"

"I've been thinking."

"About why Enrico had his brainstorm?"

"About why he wanted you and I to come to America in the first instance. I fear he may not have been entirely truthful."

"You mean, he could have found someone else? An American accountant?"

"Indubitably."

"But you've given satisfaction. You've accounted for every cent, you've even refused to give Jed Pointer more than he was entitled."

"Consider the pattern of events even before we left England. How rapid the arrangements were, how little time we had in which to check Dulce's credentials? As we now know, the actors hadn't heard of him or his production company. All they knew was their agency was happy with the contracts and money had been paid into the bank."

"So? No one's bothered because everything's been exactly the way Enrico said it would be – until he killed the dog and shot at Shirley, of course," she finished lamely. She glanced at the diner. "I do hope those two won't be much longer, I hate to think she might still be lying there."

"The actors weren't worried because they were glad of the work."

"What's wrong with that?"

"Nothing," he agreed. "You saw the possibility of a free trip in much the same light." He'd made her uneasy.

"Well?"

"Consider the film script. I'm far from being an expert but several references were completely out of date. The one about Kennedy, for instance."

"Enrico changed that line the moment Monica pointed it out."

"But the style of the whole thing. You described it as an 'old-fashioned story', with a beginning, a middle and an end. 'The way films used to be', you said."

"I don't see why you're so worried?"

"Monica discovered that Dulce had once been a location scout, a sort of general dogsbody in the industry. A contact man who tried to push scripts in the hope of gaining a small commission. I believe it could be one of those scripts we're filming."

"There's nothing wrong with it, it's a nice story."

"But would anyone make such a picture nowadays? It's all part of the feeling I have about the enterprise. Take the crew. According to Ivor it's an unusually small unit. Not normal, in other words. Lastly, wherever we go, we find that my name has been used when making any booking. Across half of America."

"Oh, well, that's US efficiency for you. As soon as you took the job, Enrico must have rung his head office – "

"Where?"

"Pardon?"

"Where did he ring? There's been no suggestion where this company of his is based. Whenever I ask, he evades the question."

"In New York, I suppose," Mavis said vaguely. "He talked about New York in the Bricklayers. Or Hollywood. That's where they make films."

"There have been too many unanswered questions."

"You're not suggesting we stop what we're doing and worry about how many office staff he's got?"

"Our first priority is to find the ranch as quickly as possible. I sincerely hope Shirley is not still there . . . "

Mavis said anxiously, "Maybe a neighbour called, or her grandson could've found her. Or Enrico may have come to his senses and taken her to the nearest Casualty department himself."

He was silent. She said suddenly, "You're worried about that damn hire car too, aren't you?"

"The thought had crossed my mind," Mr Pringle admitted. "It was my signature on the contract document. However, once we have seen to it that Shirley is in the proper hands, our rightful course is to go straight to the police and tell them everything. We can worry about the car afterwards."

She sighed. "It really is a pity, Enrico being taken queer like that. For all you're bothered I was really enjoying myself in Boulder – and looking forward to Las Vegas."

They stared at the inevitable TV pictures on the set inside the cashier's booth.

"Oh, look . . . they've reached nine million and seventy-three thousand dollars . . . No wonder Frank Sinatra's looking pleased."

"We must see to it that the actors know what's been happening."

"Yes," she said absently, "especially Monica."

"After that I suggest you and I return home as discreetly as possible. We have our airline tickets. I can hand over the balance of the float plus my receipts to one of the crew and make him responsible. Then you and I can make our way to the nearest airport."

"Yes . . ."

Mrs Bignell had recovered sufficiently from her ordeal to exhibit regret. "Just when I was within spitting distance of seeing Frank Sinatra . . ."

Two figures emerged from the diner.

"There they are, thank goodness. By the way, when I explained to Irwin the best way to the ranch is to head towards Chloride – don't they have funny names out here? – he said as it's such a long journey he'd like a contribution towards the petrol. He'll give you a receipt. It's tax deductible apparently because it's in the service of our Lord."

Mr Pringle was extremely doubtful whether the Inland Revenue would see it in that light.

It was early afternoon. John Millar presented his pass as he had every day this week when reporting for duty. The guard passed the strip through the sensor and stared at the computer.

"What's the problem?"

"I'm not getting a read-out."

"Could be because it's my new number. That one was only issued last month."

"I can see that. Got your old one?"

John affected surprise. "'Course not. I handed it in in exchange."

"You'd have to do that," the guard said grudgingly.

"You want to call my section in LA? I'm only on attachment, you know." The guard appeared even more uncertain.

"Guess not." He handed back the pass. "OK, Freeman. On your way. They're rechecking the new ones, maybe that's it."

A feeling of anger rather than fear surged through John as he strode back to his patrol car. So the pass was faulty, someone in the Family had been careless. This would be the last time he'd use the damn thing. As of midnight, Del Freeman plus pass would disappear, there'd be no more risk of being picked up, but when he was in charge, such mistakes wouldn't be *allowed* to happen.

He switched on the radio. The local station was screaming out the current total: "Ten million dollars, folks, and it's pouring in now. Don't be left out! See *your* dollars go into that bowl."

Only ten million? Some way to go. John changed the frequency and listened instead to the voices of police on patrol.

Shirley's mind was hazy; she was light-headed from loss of blood as well as the anaesthetic. The hospital nurse wasn't unsympathetic but they were very busy and the police had asked to see the patient. "You feel able to talk yet?"

"Mmm?"

"Listen, Mrs Callaghan, we know that hole in your shoulder was made by a bullet. We've patched you up but the police sent word they want to talk as soon as you're fit. I reckon you can manage to do that now, don't you?"

"Where's Sammy?"

"That the boy who brought you in?"

"My grandson."

The nurse opened the door and looked outside. "He was sitting out here for a while. He might have gone home." She was affronted at Shirley's reaction. "You can't get out of bed, Mrs Callaghan!"

"I must stop Sammy going back to the ranch – Oh!" She had slipped on the polished floor. Swearing, the nurse caught her and put out her other hand to save the drip stand.

"What the hell you do a thing like that for . . . tearing all that

nice stitching apart? Come on, let's get you back into bed."
Shirley was too weak to argue.

The nurse examined the dressing before tucking in the sheets as firmly as she could. There was a syringe in the dish. She checked the spray and held Shirley's arm firmly. "Can't have you getting upset. You'd better sleep for a little while longer."

"Please don't!"

Shirley couldn't fight it; the drug blotted out worry and consciousness alike.

Out in the parking lot, Sammy's face was creased with the effort of trying to work things out. They'd told him to wait but in that hallway, with corpse-like bodies being wheeled in and out of the operating theatre, it was too much. Besides, he had a hell of a problem about what to do with this big car. It sure was bugging him.

Suppose Mr Kuminsky came back for it? Worse, suppose Mr Freeman was with him? Sammy had no illusions about the trouble there'd be if *he* found it gone.

The nurse couldn't say when Grandma would be well enough to leave. Maybe if he went back to the ranch and when the helicopter came back, he could hand over the keys and ask Mr Kuminsky for ten dollars for gas for the pick-up? Ten dollars wouldn't mean a thing to Mr Kuminsky but it would enable Sammy to come back here. Wouldn't matter how long he had to sit and wait after that.

Relieved at solving the problem, Sammy was about to pull the tab off a Coke when he remembered. Better let the authorities know. In Sammy's world you always told someone then you couldn't be blamed afterwards. He went in search of a friendly face and found one belonging to a porter.

"I'm taking Mr Kuminsky's car back," he announced. "Tell that to my grandma. They took a bullet out of her shoulder but she's not ready to leave just yet." Without waiting for an answer, he lolloped off outside.

Back in the limousine, it occurred to him that Charlene might like a ride. Hell, he'd never have such a nice car again! Mr Kuminsky wouldn't mind. Just a little ride. Sammy would be as careful as he knew how.

At the Beaux Rêves, the two additional detectives provided by the captain had been given the task of questioning guests and staff. By now, the frenzy as to whether the target would be reached was contagious. Gambling tables were empty, everyone needed to see the dollars mount up for themselves. No one wanted to leave the excitement because of a homicide enquiry. "Judy who?" they asked. Hocht was more than content to let the two newcomers battle with the indifference.

"Where are *we* off to?" demanded Purcelle.

"We're going to wander around and get the feel of this place. The reason she was killed is right *here*, I'll swear."

"You reckon we might just bump into those two guys?"

Hocht shook his head.

"They'll stay out of sight. We've got to find the reason they did it. When we find that out, their identities might become obvious, at least, I hope so."

It was the restless part of the lieutenant's nature that made it necessary to go walkabout, Purcelle knew. He saw his own role differently.

"Those additional checks on the security passes. I guess I might call the department and see if anything has come up."

"Sure." They paused to look at the current total.

"Nearly seventeen million . . . not bad." Purcelle glanced at his watch. "Hey, at this rate Frank should do it well within the time limit."

Hocht was bleak. "God, I hope not. We need every minute we can get."

It was six o'clock. In the desert, the sun was beginning to sink behind the dunes leaving purple-black shadows behind. Far away from prying eyes, Gino was finishing his preparations. The phone began to ring inside the car.

It couldn't be Myra. Their arrangement was always for him to call her. He covered the short distance and picked up the receiver. It was Ozal.

"There's a problem. We have to meet."

Gino controlled his astonishment. "There isn't time."

"Has to be. You know where I am. Get over here fast. Stay out of sight of John." The line went dead.

Gino cursed. Ozal knew nothing of his disguised features, it would be crazy to let him see the changes now. Then he almost laughed. Ozal couldn't *see* for God's sake! But his advice was good; John might wonder why he'd done it. Gino wasn't going to take the risk, he'd be very, very careful.

He sat perfectly still, eyes closed. He knew what everyone was doing. By now, Louis and the rest must be on their way to Vegas, to film on the Strip. John would be on patrol until it was time to drive to the camper . . . he didn't bother with the rest, he knew it by heart.

But what the hell had happened? It must be bad for Ozal to call him like that. Methodical as always, Gino finished his checks before heading out of the desert back towards town.

Jed Pointer was easily angered but this time Ivor Henry agreed with him. Their hotel rooms in Las Vegas were above a casino and across the road from a bus depot. "Room free with breakfast," Ivor read with incredulity. "What is this, a Salvation Army hostel? Where's Pringle? I want to complain."

"The hotel part must be subsidised by the gambling, I suppose," said Monica, "and I can't see either him or Mavis, can you?"

The reception area was part of the vast dark cavern that made up the ground floor. Armed guards walked along lines of dedicated women who sat pushing dollar coins into hundreds of fruit machines as though their lives depended on it. Overhead was the inevitable TV screen. The noise deafened them.

"When I do see Pringle, I shall certainly have something to say," Ivor raised his voice. "Agreeing to us staying here, for crying out loud!"

"Well, as we are, and I have a key with a number on it," Monica scooped up her shoulder-bag, "I propose to get some rest. Do we know the make-up calls?"

"They said they'd come and see us in our rooms," Clarissa replied, "in about an hour."

"What's wrong with the caravan?"

"That's been driven direct to the first location, on the Strip. That's where the crew have gone too." Clarissa couldn't hide her eagerness. Monica smiled.

"I must say I'm quite looking forward to seeing that. I wonder if it's as exciting as the postcards. Bye for the present."

★

It was dusk. Stars hung bright in the desert sky but though she stared at them Shirley's gaze was focused inside the hospital room. The side-effect of the drug had induced a vision of Cal, so vivid she felt she could touch him. An ache brought back memories and now her cheeks were damp.

When the nurse next came to check the drip, she would ask again about Sammy. She would agree to talk to the police, in fact it was urgent that she did so. It was the only way to protect him.

There was a shuffling. A face peered round the door. The porter had taken his time. "You somebody's grandma?"

"Sammy? Is he there?"

"The kid wanted you to know he'd taken the car back. To a Mr . . . K something."

"Kuminsky."

"Something like that. OK?" He saw her shiver. "You want me to call the nurse?"

"And the police, if they're still about."

"Ain't no police, lady. I'll find someone though." He disappeared.

The countdown clock showed less than six hours to go. The golden bowl was close to overflowing. The orchestral climax was tremendous as the Star commanded, "Empty it again!" Below the stage the code was tapped into the control box, the curved cover rolled into position and then rolled back again; the dollars had disappeared as if by magic. "Come on, folks, it's time to fill it up again. We've got to try just a little bit harder. You can do it, I know you can."

Up in the control room, a cue light came on.

"Yes?" asked the director. An operator among those manning the bank of phones answered.

"It's a big donation – one million dollars – the guy wants to tell Frank about it himself. Coming in live now . . . from Singapore."

"OK." The director called to the graphic operator, "Are you hearing the name?"

"Yes." Her fingers typed automatically as the voice in her ear spelled it out. "Oh my!"

The director pressed the override button.

"Stand-by, Frank. This one's from Singapore and it's big." He released the button, and asked, "Is he hearing it?"

The sound director nodded. "Cue him."

Without losing his professional flow, the Star announced, "And now, from far away in the east, from Singapore, ladies and gentlemen, with a donation of – wait for it! A donation of – one million dollars! In a minute we'll give you the name, but first let's see those dollars fill the bowl! A million bucks, how about that?"

Two security men wheeled forward a large steel container and proceeded to unlock it. A beautiful girl with a rapturous cleavage began tossing wads of hundred-dollar bills light-heartedly and the onlookers were ecstatic.

Listening to his ear-piece, the Star heard, "You pronounce the name SUN KOO FUK, Frank. No kidding. SUN KOO FUK." He spun on his heel and spoke briefly into his slaved camera.

"May you not be telling me a lie," and without losing his smile, turned back into the wide shot. "Let's hear it loud enough to reach the most generous man in Singapore, our thanks to . . . " he confirmed it on the hastily scribbled cue card, "to Mr Sun Koo Fuk!" and only those backstage could see the crossed fingers. "Give him an extra cheer." With a name like that he deserved it. "One million dollars for all those kids! Let's talk to him, let's hear Mr – Sun – tell us about the donation."

"So what happened after you found the light didn't work, Mrs Callaghan?"

Over the hospital bed was a dim lamp that showed Shirley's hands but left her face in shadow. The detective was in darkness, apart from his notebook, his questions were disembodied. Nearer the door, a woman police officer listened, her eyes on Shirley's face. The woman looked so ill!

"I tripped over Bomber's body – that's the dog. I knew he was dead. It was dark but you could smell the blood."

"Uh–huh."

"Mrs Bignell and Mr Pringle came running when they heard me shout. I got the other light on, the switch is beside the dresser, and there he was." She shuddered. "He was big . . . he had this gun – "

"Did you recognise him?" Shirley's hands were tight as she tried to stop shaking. It was important to get it right for Sammy's sake.

"I didn't. I'd never seen him before but *they* knew him, and he certainly recognised them. I still can't understand it. I've tried and tried to work it out; why should there be a gunman, why should two people I'd met by chance only hours before happen to know him – "

"OK. Don't upset yourself – "

"But it was seeing *them* which made him mad," she urged them to understand. "He couldn've cared less about me. OK, he fired but by then he was wild, out of his mind." She paused. Had she been coherent? She didn't want to land her new friends in trouble but if this was nothing to do with Sammy, they must take the consequences.

"I've been thinking . . . They must've met him since they landed in the States. Mrs Bignell told me they'd never been here before, they didn't know anyone. It could be coincidence, I guess . . . " She lifted her shoulders then winced. "I'm certain they weren't expecting to see him, nor he them."

"You think it might be the man who contacted your grandson?"

"I don't know . . . " the pain was making it difficult. "It wasn't the same *name* . . . Sammy always talked about a Mr Kuminsky and a Mr Freeman. I think Mavis screamed 'Enrico'; she was really worked up, it was the name she called the film producer. None of it makes sense. I've lost a lot of blood . . . maybe I haven't been thinking straight."

"Take it easy, we're nearly through, Mrs Callaghan." Shirley managed a watery smile. "Do you remember what happened after he'd shot you?"

"He left me there while he dragged them outside. I heard a car start up."

"Did you see the make?"

"He'd hidden it round the back. I heard him bumping both of them down the steps. When he started dragging me through to Sammy's room I passed out, it hurt so much. When I came round I was in the closet. It was so quiet." Shirley couldn't hold back remembered fears, "I thought I was going to die!"

"OK," he soothed. "Is there anything else you want to tell me?"

"It must be to do with our old barn, nothing else makes any sense . . . I'm so worried for Sammy. Supposing it *is* drugs? You won't blame him for any of it, will you?" The detective stood up.

"Now listen, Mrs Callaghan, we'll go take a look at the barn. If Sammy's at home, we'll have a talk with him, too."

"It's not his fault. It's my fault for worrying him about the bank loan."

"Could be that the rental's a legitimate business. The reason the gunman was there could be something else. We'll find out."

"Tell Sammy . . . "

"Yes?"

"To feed the stock. And check their water. The trough leaks, it always needs filling up on Sundays."

"It's only Saturday, Mrs Callaghan, but we'll remind him."

It had been a long drive in Irwin's lorry. Enoch's prophet was barely civil when Mavis called out excitedly, "That's it! There's the turning to the ranch. Shirley showed us that yellow marker stone, it practically glows in the dark, doesn't it? Oh, sorry. I forgot about the potholes."

Big Joe jumped out and knelt beside the front wheel, shining his torch at various joints along the shaft. "Don't look like there's too much damage. Take it easy, Irwin. How much further, ma'am?"

Mavis peered into the dark.

"About two hundred yards. There aren't any lights on, which is a pity. Perhaps Sammy isn't back yet?" The driver appeared reluctant to restart and to encourage him, she urged, "Buck up, Irwin, we're nearly there."

"It's the killer I'm thinking about. A maniac – "

"Oh, bollocks! You're talking about Enrico Dulce. He's cuddly. Something went wrong inside his brain, that's all. Mind you, if he is still in there, he's going to get a piece of my mind. Now start driving. God's on your side, remember. He must be with all that preaching you do for him."

Unconvinced, Irwin switched off the lights and drove as slowly and as silently as possible.

The outline of the ranch began to appear. Inside the cab, the atmosphere grew tense. It was Mr Pringle who broke it. He saw something which made him cry out.

"Isn't that . . . It is! Oh, golly, look what's happened to our hire car."

"Ssh!" begged Irwin. "Keep your voice down, that gunman might hear!"

"Oh, dear!" Mavis was equally loud. "It must have been in an accident." She reached over and flicked on the headlights, deaf to Irwin's frightened squawk.

The uncertain beam showed clearly the dent in the limousine's door, the stove-in front wing and a torn-off bumper.

"It's exactly where we left it," she said, amazed, "but something must've happened."

From his hiding place, still shaking with terror at the thought of retribution, Sammy watched the brightly painted truck pull up. Four strangers got out. The woman had red hair, just like the picture on the side. Was it a circus? Was she going to drive that chariot?

She went straight over to the car and ran her hand over the dent, tut-tutting and saying something to the man who followed her. He was dressed in old-fashioned clothes and acted like he was really upset.

Suddenly the woman said, "There's no use dithering. We've got to find Shirley and take her to hospital, I don't care if Enrico's here or not."

The two other men hung back but the woman marched straight up the steps and in through the fly-screen, followed by the old-fashioned man. Hearing her speak, Sammy realised she must be one of the Brits his grandma had told him about.

She was shouting, "If Shirley's here, we've got to find her. Hallo? Anyone at home?"

She had Big Joe's torch and flashed it round the room. Sammy heard her say, "The dog's gone, thank goodness . . . and someone's cleaned up the mess. I don't believe there's anyone else about."

Sammy had buried Bomber. Sobbing his heart out, he'd dug a grave in the corner plot beside Grandad Cal. Seemed like the only thing he could do for his best friend. He'd sat on the verandah for a while after that, waiting for Mr Kuminsky to arrive.

Eventually, the thought of what Mr Freeman might do overcame him. Sammy climbed up into his old hiding place among the rafters. He had discovered it when he was a kid. Now, quiet as a mouse, he watched as the red-headed woman and her companion re-emerged. The man called out, "It's all right,

Irwin, Dulce isn't here, neither is Shirley. Some good Samaritan must have called." The two hiding behind the truck straightened up and began behaving like they'd never been frightened of anything in their lives.

As Sammy continued to watch, the lady and man walked round the limo again and stared. He was shaking his head. "I cannot understand, I cannot believe the evidence of my eyes. This car looks as if it's been hit by a rhinoceros."

Sammy could have told them, he'd been there when it happened. He'd been in the passenger seat when Charlene had tried a turn too close to a parked gasoline truck. She'd been mighty sorry. The driver had come out – boy, he'd been big. He'd yelled at them. Charlene'd started crying, so had Sammy. The driver had threatened to punch his head off so Sammy'd jumped back in the car and Charlene had done the same.

He'd taken her home after that. Then he'd driven here and parked on the same spot, hoping when he arrived, Mr Kuminsky might not notice the damage in the dark.

Now these two were acting like the car belonged to them, which baffled Sammy completely. It was all too complicated and he was worn out. Draped uncomfortably over the beams, he slept.

Chapter Seven

The woman looked from one to the other with a languorous sweep of her eyes. Emptying ashtrays and cleaning floors in the Beaux Rêves was mindless work. Being interviewed was much better. For one thing, it meant sitting down. And if she looked over the lieutenant's shoulder, she could still see what was happening down in the ballroom.

They'd raised over twenty-two million at the last count. Wouldn't be long before they reached the total but she couldn't get inside to see it happen, it was packed out with rich folk down there. She wondered, idly, if her information was worth a reward.

The two police officers were discussing something out of earshot; she was content to wait and watch the screen.

"This is the only one we've come up with so far, Lieutenant, but you said to tell you the moment we got a hint of anything. Jimmy's still checking the rest of the staff." Gary Hocht nodded. This detective was keen, it was good to have him on the team.

"This woman reckoned she couldn't get through to one particular in-house number?"

"Right. She said she needed to make a call to the director in charge of facilities. His department sees to everything from garbage disposal to replacement light fitments. These people have to phone his office if anything's wrong. If their machines break down, for instance. Everything gets logged."

"OK." Gary Hocht moved forward to speak to the woman. "I'd like you to tell me what you just told my colleague here. Take your time." Sure thing.

"Well . . . Ah was cleaning out the trash on the mezzanine that mornin' . . . ma machine got all jammed up. Ah wanted to tell the boss. Ah couldn't get through. Kep' on trying . . . " She shrugged massively, "Jes' no use at all."

"Was the number ringing out?"

"Uh-huh." She nodded. "It was busy at first, then it jes' keep ringing like there was no one there. Always is, though. Always got through before."

Hocht turned to the detective. "Is there only the one phone using that number?"

"Yes, on the desk in the director's office. The management like one guy to be responsible for the whole operation. There's three of them to cover twenty-four hours, always one on shift. If he has to go to the john, his secretary answers. It's a busy department, it even includes the fountains and water gardens – "

"We're not interested in outside," Hocht interrupted. "It's got to be in the building." The woman continued to look dreamily past his left shoulder at the TV.

"You tried several times."

"Yeah."

"Did you get through eventually?"

"No."

"Do you remember *when* you made the calls?"

It had been around lunchtime. "Ah told the next girl when she took over to keep on tryin'. That machine still wasn't workin'." Hocht looked at the detective.

"We've spoken to her. Everything was back to normal by two o'clock and she got through to the right office." Hocht was on his feet.

"Guess we know where to look . . . even if we don't yet know what for. Where does the guy hang out?"

"Second floor."

They were half-way to the door when the woman called plaintively, "Hey . . . ain't that worth something, mister?" Hocht paused. She was shabby enough.

"Here."

"Thanks." She stuffed the five–dollar bill in her cleavage and rose, reluctantly.

"Guess Ah'd better get back." Hocht held the door open and she sashayed through genteelly. "You're a real gen'leman."

The facilities director on the current shift was from Milwaukee;

he answered Hocht's questions before the lieutenant had finished speaking as if time was too precious to waste. Yes, he had been on duty on that particular morning. No, he hadn't received any calls around lunchtime. Yes, it was surprising. Usually there was a steady flow, particularly following the invasion of the TV people who had disrupted the entire casino operation.

From his attitude Hocht judged that the man was not particularly concerned about raising money for charity. He was one of the many lured to Vegas by the prospect of a crock of gold, still convinced after plenty of evidence to the contrary, that he could make his fortune.

Hocht asked if anyone had complained of not being able to get through to the number. The director thought about it briefly. As far as he could remember, only one other person. Fortunately, not for any serious reason. "A guest let the bathtub run over, it soaked the ceiling beneath; happens all the time."

Without explaining why, Hocht indicated the phone and told him that someone might have diverted his calls. The man stared.

"What the hell for?"

"That we don't yet know," the lieutenant admitted. "Someone presumably wanted to pretend to be you. What powers would that give him?"

"Oh, my God!" The confident persona began to falter.

"You remembered something?"

"The security people . . . "

"Yes?"

"We hold duplicates of staff passes on file up here, with photos attached. Not the office clerks or croupiers, just the maintenance people, but there's a high turn-over in a place like this."

"So?"

"So Security phone this number to check, especially since the appeal began. We've a whole new bunch of guards who don't even know the regular staff, they can't be expected to recognise replacements."

"Shit!"

"But why?" The director couldn't bring himself to face the possibility so Hocht spelled it out.

"Someone who knew there would be twenty-three million dollars on the premises tonight, perhaps? In used bills. Who might be interested in acquiring that money? Who might use this office number to authorise members of his gang to enter this casino as staff, and be in position for a heist?" The face opposite had gone white.

"You mean, stage a robbery? But that's impossible!"

"You think so? That's an interesting theory. All I know is a woman called Judy Beeker, who deputised for the regular operator in your communications room, may have switched relays. Whatever she did, she died for it that same night."

"My God . . . " The man stared at the screen in the corner of the office. "What's going to happen now?"

"I wish we knew. Are you responsible for the whole of the technical aspects of this building?"

"More or less. We don't have anything to do with window cleaning, that's contracted out, but we do look after power, gas, cleaning, damage to the interior – "

"If someone wanted to interfere, like stop the appeal happening long enough to grab those millions of dollars, what would he do? Where would be the most effective weak link?"

The man was speechless and Hocht looked pointedly at the clock. "Start thinking real fast. We need the answer. He'd have to do something big, wouldn't he, like plant a bomb. Where would he put that?"

The man from Milwaukee began to jabber. "But . . . this place has been checked over and over. We're falling over the security people, there's so many of them. My staff have their passes checked every time they come and go. If there's any doubt, the guards call me."

The detective interjected quietly, "Sir, we've been assuming whoever we're after must have used the pass just once. But suppose he or she is still in the building, part of the current temporary staff, and not drawing attention to himself?"

Hocht frowned.

"You mean he or she went out . . . and came back? Just used the diverted number on one occasion? Why?" Before Hocht could reply, the manager said, puzzled, "What I don't understand is that I was using that goddamn phone myself that morning."

"Of course you were," Hocht was sharp. "We never said she tampered with the line, she simply switched the number. When you rang out there was no reason *you* couldn't make a call; it was people trying to reach you who had the problem. But this number was back to normal by two o'clock, we're all agreed on that."

"Of course." The manager was annoyed at being stupid, "Plenty of people phoned me that afternoon."

"Was the office left unmanned at all?"

"God no, not this week. More than my job's worth."

"Have there been any queries about staff passes?" the detective asked curiously.

"Are you kidding? People hand passes around the family, goes on all the time. One of the kitchen hands feels sick, asks his brother to turn up instead. Christ, this place would fall apart if we didn't let that happen. We usually know who they are. If the face doesn't match the photograph, we usually know the families." Hocht nodded.

"Have you spotted any strangers lately?"

The man snorted. "With Frank Sinatra on the premises? It may not surprise you to learn one or two have been female."

"None of them was blind by any chance?" Hocht asked off-handedly.

"Hell, no. None of the lady guests anyway." He was distracted by a new total suddenly appearing on the screen followed by a close-up of dollar bills spilling out of the bowl. "Hey, look at that . . . they've nearly got there! The only blind guy comes here is the piano tuner."

"What!"

As if on cue, the picture on the screen changed to a glistening white baby grand. The Star walked into shot and began introducing a new act. In the office, the three of them stared as the singer, young, fresh and blonde, leaned against the piano and pouted prettily at them.

"That piano?" asked Hocht in a flat tone. But the manager was beginning to recover.

"We're not idiots. That blind guy has been here hundreds of times. He's the regular piano tuner."

"Tall, bald, in his sixties?" Hocht reeled off, "with a companion, a sharp dresser, late twenties."

"No, comes here by himself." The manager had regained his poise. "Besides, that piano's been checked by experts. Every single item in that ballroom is squeaky clean – "

"When was his last visit?"

"God, I don't know. It's a regular contract. They supply tuners two or three times a week, sometimes twice a day if it's a big name topping the bill."

Hocht was staring. "You mean there's more than one blind guy comes here?"

"I couldn't say. There's this company who provide a 24-hour service to several casinos – one of their tuners is blind, that's all. Can't tell you his name, you'd have to phone the company."

Hocht spoke rapidly.

"Ring headquarters, tell Purcelle to get back here and bring help. Find out if that guy came here on a regular basis and was in the building recently . . . "

"Sure, I understand."

"It may not be to do with Mrs Beeker but it's a lead and I think we should follow it. Tell that to the captain if he queries anything." The detective moved swiftly.

To the manager, Hocht said, "Get me that tuning company number." As the man flicked through a card index, Hocht asked, "How long would it take your maintenance staff to examine every square inch? I'm thinking of service ducts, cabling, hatches, things like that. Anything which connects with the ballroom." The manager was astonished.

"To do a thorough job, a couple of days. It took the security firm a week."

"We've got less than one and a half hours. Let's get started."

As he approached the camper, parked inconspicuously in the corner of the lot, Gino paused. There was no sign of John, which was to be expected. Gino waited a full minute nonetheless, before moving up to the vehicle and tapping on the door.

As he entered, he kept a space between himself and Ozal. He didn't want a friendly hand reaching out to touch either his clothes or his hair. It was uncanny how little information Ozal needed to guess at a changed appearance.

There was an unpleasant surprise: one of Ozal's team hunched over the radio transmitter. Gino's stomach lurched, he'd forgotten the man would be here. He remembered him vaguely, from one of the Family reunions.

Would the guy describe the changes or assume it to be part of the plan? It was too late to worry about that now. Belatedly, he realised Ozal looked unfamiliar – he was wearing a patrol cop's jacket – what the hell for? There wasn't enough time to find out.

"I have to leave as soon as possible – "

"Sit down. This won't take long but you have to understand. It's serious. It's all gone wrong, Gino. Very, very wrong. We have to change the plan."

Gino's heart began to thud; before he could stop himself, he asked, "Is it Louis?"

"Louis, and John. He was an idiot. He killed Judy Beeker. There was no need – she wouldn't have betrayed anyone – but the police have already found the body. Guess you haven't been listening to the radio or you'd have heard."

"I've been busy."

"Louis is up to something, I don't know what."

"Is he still doing the filming?"

"Oh, sure. He and John are both doing what they have to, they aren't that stupid. I intend to speak to Louis before he leaves for the Strip though, to explain the necessary changes. I'll double-check then that everything's as per schedule." Ozal broke off to speak briefly to the radio operator who took off his cans and went outside.

"Listen, Gino, neither Louis nor John know we've spotted them. I realise they're members of the Family but we can't take the risk. They have to be taken out. Someone else is going to take care of John but we want you to handle Louis." There was a pause. Ozal was waiting for him to speak.

"What about Beth?"

Ozal replied smoothly, "Forget about her, Gino. Forget about friendship, I know how much it means but forget about everything except your own skin. That's what's important now. Find out what Louis's been doing because we have to know that before you kill him."

"It won't work, Ozal. Nothing to do with how I feel but according to the plan, I don't meet up with Louis again, remember."

"This is where everything changes. It stays the same up to the point when you arrive at the ranch. That's when I want you to *remain* there instead of leaving in the helicopter with John. And I want you to off-load *all* the boxes, not just the ones you'll have taped up. The whole pay-out is going to take place there instead of what we arranged."

"What if John won't accept that? Are you saying he should leave all our shares behind or do you intend he should take his with him in the helicopter?"

Ozal's voice was hard this time. "All you have to worry about is killing Louis, Gino. Apart from seeing those boxes go in the barn, you can leave the rest to me. There's a gun in the middle drawer of the unit. It's loaded." Gino searched as bidden. "There's a spare clip nearer the back."

"I have it. Ozal, John won't let me off-load the money without a fight."

If John had already killed the Beeker woman he'd be suspicious as hell of any last minute changes, even if Gino could claim they'd been ordered by Ozal. And if John found out what was to happen to Louis, wouldn't he guess he might be next on the list?

As if reading his thoughts, Ozal said, "You won't be alone with John. I shall be there."

"In the helicopter?" Things were changing so rapidly, Gino couldn't take it in. Ozal smiled thinly. There was no need for him to know too much.

"Now listen, this is how it goes: Louis will be at the barn. When the camera crew tell him to call me, I shall explain we've had to make changes. Louis doesn't know where the barn is but I'll give him the map reference. He'll drive over. You'll already be there. When you've done what you have to, take your share of the money and use his car. Get rid of it as soon as possible and get the hell out. Just make one phone call, use the New York number. Let the Family know what Louis's been up to. All you and Myra have to do after that is disappear. Understood?"

"Yes."

"One last thing: leave the money for your boys to collect, as per the arrangement. Put the frighteners on the old lady and her grandson so they don't call the cops before everyone's gotten clear. It's not good but it's the best we can do."

Not good! Gino thought it was the worst scenario he'd ever come across. Give the old lady a really good chance to get a look at him? A top to toe description for the cops? Who was Ozal trying to kid! He was silent.

"On your way, Gino."

"Sure," he said. He accidentally brushed past the other chair on his way to the door. Ozal sniffed.

"Changed your aftershave?" The lacquer Myra had given him to keep the curly hairstyle intact was scented.

"It's part of being Kuminsky, something for people to remember him by," he said quickly. "I'm junking it after tonight."

"Subtle," Ozal sounded approving. "An interesting touch, Gino."

As he left, Gino didn't know whether the smile was genuine or his death warrant. Outside, there was no sign of the radio operator but he'd be watching. Somewhere.

Gino drove fast. He'd covered ten miles before he pulled off the road and opened the window. In contrast to the blackness all around, Las Vegas blazed with light in his rear-view mirror. Not for much longer. Gino took little pleasure in that thought now.

He'd been a fool. He'd allowed himself to be beguiled by Ozal, who'd convinced him he was the only one to make his precious plan work. Gino had been swept along by the intricacies of getting it right. He'd been used. Now the Family had given him the dirtiest job of all, to kill a friend.

The plan hadn't been so smart; it had taken very little for it to fall apart. Louis Carlson had lost his nerve, so what? They'd realised that much in New York. Why hadn't Ozal found a replacement before this?

Gino answered his own question: they needed Louis, that's why. Filming on the Strip was the vital distraction during the last few seconds. Louis's ability to behave like a producer, his knowledge of how to direct, were essential, as were the Brits, to muddy the waters still further.

As for why John killed Judy Beeker, wasn't that equally obvious? A deliberate stepping out of line, a flouting of Ozal's absolute authority. His nephew intended to become head of the Family. Killing the phone operator was to convince the rest of them he meant business.

Gino and Myra would have no future if that happened. They would have to disappear but there was the rest of tonight to get through first.

Would *he* be given his share? A pay-out at the barn could be a trap. And as for sticking around when every police officer in the State would be out searching for them, that was ludicrous.

Suppose Louis took too long finding the ranch? Just how long was Gino supposed to wait? Suppose he was there with Louis's bullet-riddled body when the cops arrived? He might not have time to hide the corpse. As for the old lady and her grandson, they weren't likely to stay quiet once shooting began.

Suddenly it seemed one hell of a crazy operation. Gino swung the car back on to the road. He had to think fast. From now on he would play a lone hand, his own. Being the patsy wasn't his style.

At the ranch, the first decision had been to wait until Sammy returned but several hours had passed and Mavis was restless. The phone wasn't working but as Mr Pringle pointed out, they didn't know which hospital to ring anyway.

She had managed to cobble a meal together out of tins, promising herself she would repay Shirley by leaving dollars in the jar on the mantelpiece, and Big Joe gave it as his opinion that he and Irwin would stay the night out in the yard.

"We have to let the radiator cool off," he explained. "It got real shook up on the dirt track out there. I reckon the filters need cleaning too before we start her up again. We need to do that in daylight."

He showed her round Irwin's truck. In the back was everything a man needed "for the service of the Lord", including bedding rolls and a canvas awning which stretched over a frame and could be attached to the side of the lorry.

"Me and Irwin have been taking the word to sinners before, see. He's a sensation when it comes to preaching, yes sir!" Big Joe puffed out his chest in the familiar way. Mrs Bignell found herself wondering if the prophet shaved before such an important event, or at the very least, put on a clean T-shirt.

Big Joe continued, "We put up a stand. Irwin gets up there and closes his eyes. If we're lucky, the word of Enoch comes down direct to him from heaven. We made a hundred and fifty dollars in Peach Springs, Arizona, when that happened one time. Irwin talked about the devil whore so you could almost smell her fiery breath."

"Fancy," said Mrs Bignell.

Sammy had remained in his hidey-hole, dozing fitfully and waiting for Mr Kuminsky to return. He'd lost interest in the four strangers wandering about below. They were nothing to do with the barn. Presumably Grandma had invited them.

He tried not to think that Grandma might have died by the time he got back to the hospital. She'd been so covered in blood, just like Bomber. He could see the spade below that he'd used for digging the grave; it hurt even to look at it.

Sammy sucked his thumb. He would stay where he was until everyone had gone away. He'd be safe so long as he remained out of sight.

Mavis found the ranch depressing. The lamp showed only too plainly the level of Shirley's poverty and she was sufficiently upset by it not to want to watch television.

"All those millions and she obviously hasn't got a bean. I feel as if we're prying, just by being in here. Let's wait on the verandah," she suggested, "it's a beautiful night. Very warm for the time of year."

Mr Pringle's battered muscles were protesting, all he wanted was a hot bath followed by a nice warm bed. He wondered if he dare suggest they borrow Shirley's, but followed obediently. Parked outside, under the awning, the prophet and his disciple slumbered peacefully.

The old chair creaked under Mavis's weight. She was silent for a while, gazing at a distant solitary truck on the highway.

"I should go mad living here, wouldn't you? Especially after Salford. It's so lonely."

"It would be exciting at the beginning. A new life, full of hope."

"Oh yes, at the beginning. Shirley said she couldn't get over all the lovely fresh food when she first came out, especially after rationing. It was all right until her son and his wife had their accident. I think she nearly went potty when her husband died as well. She obviously loved him.

"The farm's getting her down these days. She says she can't manage it on her own." Mavis sighed. "I can't think of anything worse, can you? Losing everyone like that, frightened of the future." Her companion didn't reply. "I told her she should think of returning to England."

"Yes, I heard you."

"It's not as though she's got that many friends out here. She's been too isolated."

"There's still the grandson."

Mavis considered. "I don't suppose he'd be any worse off. She might find more help with him back home. Over here, you need money to breathe, it seems to me."

"We shouldn't interfere," he said uneasily. "A chance acquaintanceship doesn't give us the right."

"Oh, blow that. Shirley's lying in some hospital, probably worrying herself silly over affording the treatment – "

"Mavis, we are not using any more of the float. If that's what you were about to suggest, please don't. That money doesn't belong to us, it's a loan from Dulce's company."

She turned on him haughtily. "I have my barleycard, thanks very much, and I'm not sitting out here any longer. Instead of star-gazing, you and I ought to be out there looking for her. I vote we don't wait for Sammy. He must have decided to spend the night with friends and Shirley's almost bound to be in Boulder City. Big Joe said that's where they'd take her."

"We can't be certain."

"What about telling Monica and the rest of them about Enrico? You said that was important. Where will they be by now? If we can't find her, at least we can do one good deed." Mr Pringle forced his tired brain to work it out.

"They must be in Las Vegas."

"Lucky devils," said Mavis crossly. "Come on. I'll never sleep till I know Shirley's all right. Let's take the car and go to Boulder City. It doesn't matter about the damage. I'll drive. You can park it in that E–Z place. You can manage that much, can't you?"

"I expect so," said Mr Pringle humbly.

"We'll ask the hotel where the hospital is, they're bound to know. We can use our room to wash and change. I need a clean pair of knickers – "

"Just a minute. What about Irwin and Joe?"

"We'll leave them a message. They can explain to Sammy when he turns up. They're perfectly safe where they are." She paused, "There's another thing . . . "

"Yes?" He was apprehensive.

"I want a doctor to take a look at you when we find the Casualty department. You were unconscious for far too long this morning. You had me worried."

He was alarmed but for a different reason.

"Mavis, I don't think we can afford medical treatment. I doubt whether Dulce took out any insurance."

"We can have your head X-rayed," she insisted. "Mrs Ellis had to pay for one of those when she had her plastic hip. It cost seventy quid and we can manage that much, surely?"

There was no point in arguing. Mavis was impatient and she was right; they had a duty to discover what had happened. In some obscure way Mr Pringle felt responsible. If they hadn't come to America, Enrico Dulce might not have turned up and killed the unfortunate animal . . . Or would he? It was too complicated. He went to the sink and dowsed his head to prepare for the journey.

As they drove, Mavis pondered. "I wonder how the appeal's doing?"

"Would you like me to find it on the radio?"

"Please." He pressed a couple of buttons.

"Twenty-two million, five hundred thousand and thirty!" screamed a voice.

"How lovely!" She began to perk up. "He's bound to make it. There's only one hour left and everyone will want to help."

"Most commendable." Mr Pringle could afford to be generous now he wasn't enduring the hordes on the pavements of Las Vegas.

"I bet Mrs Ellis is enjoying every minute. It'll be dreadful at the Bricklayers when she gets back. Did I ever tell you, she's the worst show-off I've ever met."

In the police department, there was less urgency over Shirley Callaghan's problems. It was late. "Whoever he was, the gunman won't be at the ranch. It's been hours since it happened and she heard him drive away."

"If those two Brits were in the trunk, I don't see what we can do about it. We don't know what sort of car he's got, there's no point in setting up road blocks."

"Specially as we don't know which way he headed. Could be half-way to Vermont by now."

"The grandson's taken off, there's no one else we can ask. We'll go take a look in daylight."

"That'll be soon enough," the other agreed. "How's the appeal?"

"Frankie's doing great. Last I heard, he'd nearly made it."

"Fifty-five minutes to go, right?"

"Right."

Gino was relaxed. He could see his destination on the horizon. He only needed fifteen minutes once he got there. Ozal's gun was in his pocket. His own was in the glove compartment. He debated which one he should use, now he'd decided what to do.

In the television control room at the Beaux Rêves the final hour was being disrupted. The carefully arranged programme had been swept aside. As always happens with success the sponsors had crowded in and were attempting to take over the proceedings.

"OK, listen everybody, we've got the total promised now. Keep all the pledges stood-by and bring them in one at a time, nice and slow. No point in hurrying the result, we want to hit it on the button at midnight. We'll use that sexy tall girl at the finish. Keep her out of sight then wheel her in with the final hundred dollars which she can put in the bowl all by herself. She and Frank can go into a clinch."

Another sponsor, even more excited, yelled, "We'll take an extra commercial during the next break, we've got the biggest audience in the world. We can plug our own product for Chrissake!"

"Is Madonna ready? Let's go into the break, finish with the pack shot and she can back-announce how happy she is to use it!"

"Great idea! Check with Frank he's agreeable. Keep that graphic flashing with the total. Let's get to twenty-two and a half million by eleven-thirty and build up real slow from there. What's the next shot?"

"Why ask me?" the director said tiredly.

"Hey, this is no time to freak out. My wife's on the front row. Her dress cost two thousand bucks – "

"The hell with that!" another yelled. "My wife's had her buttocks fixed – they look fantastic! Take a shot of those."

Chapter Eight

11.35 p.m. on the 17th

Despite his disgust at the squalid hotel, Ivor Henry was determined to give of his best. Monica had turned in a real performance in Boulder City, eclipsing them with the emotion she'd managed to inject into banal lines; even the crew had been impressed.

It was a challenge; Ivor considered his reflection. He'd fallen into the habit of using tricks rather than exploring the words in order to give that little bit extra. Monica was dedicated. She'd done nothing but work ever since they'd arrived. Only three days ago, it felt like a lifetime.

He leaned closer. He'd demanded a warmer skin tone, he couldn't afford to look his age, not yet, and there were some nasty little lines developing round his mouth.

Tonight, he would match her performance. He half wished they could go back and retake some of the earlier stuff. No matter. The scene that mattered was still to come.

It was a bind having to change here and the wardrobe girl was too perfunctory by half, which annoyed him.

"I cannot remember whether I was wearing this jacket or carrying it?" She looked blank. "At the end of the preceding scene? Would you kindly check your continuity notes." She behaved as though she hadn't heard which made him acerbic. "I realise it may not seem important to you but it's a matter of professionalism to me to get it right. I don't want to waste time querying the matter when we're out on the Strip."

In front of a crowd, was what he meant. She made a show of consulting her notebook.

"It was slung round your shoulders."

"At the end of the shot? I had a feeling I slipped it off and folded

118

it over my arm as Monica went past up the steps." She shrugged.

"So carry it, it's not important."

Not important? It was his turn to stare. "Do you realise how few cutaways Enrico's filmed so far? The edit's going to be a nightmare as it is without any unnecessary errors."

The girl checked her watch for the third time.

"For God's sake stop doing that, we're not going to be late," he cried pettishly.

"Enrico's waiting downstairs."

"So you said before. I must say I think he's being very tolerant. Pringle ought to have been here, organising everything. I cannot imagine what's happened to him and Mavis."

She flicked him a quick look, interested. "You don't know where they are?"

"I do not. In Boulder, when Monica and I asked, Enrico said they'd come on ahead but I've seen no sign of them."

She preceded him down the corridor and into the lift. On the ground floor, the other three actors stood beside untended fruit machines. The silence was uncanny; no one was pushing dollars into slots, everyone crowded round the television instead.

"Ready?" Monica smiled at him.

"I hope so." Ivor was experiencing unwelcome stage fright. "I trust we can have a proper run-through before we go for a take tonight. Somewhere private."

"We'll ask if we can do a word rehearsal in the caravan."

"Good idea," Ivor said gratefully. "Where's Enrico?"

"Making a phone call. The cameraman said there was a query, something to do with the arrangements."

Ivor frowned. "That confounded idiot Pringle really should be here . . . " He caught sight of another tight face. "How are you feeling, young Clarissa?"

"Frightfully nervous. It's all very well these guards walking about with guns," her voice, clear and bell-like, rose with indignation, "but when you're in the street and simply ask directions to a coffee shop, you don't expect a man's hand to slide towards his holster, do you?" Hostile faces were looking in their direction.

"We'd better start making a move," Monica said tactfully.

"It really is too bad of Pringle. That limo was intended for us, not for gadding about. I suppose we'll all have to crowd into Enrico's car."

"We're using taxis. Parking anywhere near the Strip is a problem, especially tonight."

Ivor gazed resentfully at the group glued to the screen.

"All this hysteria because of money."

"It is a good cause," Monica reminded him. "I was watching earlier. Mounds of dollars! It brings out the worst. I found myself thinking: if only I could get my hands on some of that!"

"Fat chance. Look at those guards round that vulgar gold bath."

"Where is everybody?" Jed Pointer had emerged out of his trance. Monica glanced at her watch.

"Enrico's cutting it fine. He said we had to be on the Strip by eleven forty-five. Oh, there he is."

Ivor thought he'd never seen anyone change so much in such a short time. In London Dulce had been the big, genial American; bonhomie personified. Now he looked to be at breaking point. His breathing was ragged as though he'd been running.

Ivor said involuntarily, "It's too bad of Pringle, leaving you to cope."

"No time to talk – " Dulce was shooing them through the doors into the night heat. "C'm on, get inside, all of you." He sat in beside the driver.

From the back of the taxi Ivor noticed the rings of dried sweat on Dulce's shirt. He'd been wearing the same clothes at Boulder City, and he hadn't shaved. Ivor's nostrils wrinkled. What had the man been doing? He couldn't have been on the phone all the time? It wasn't fair or reasonable; how could *he* give of his best without the director feeling fresh to inspire him?

"This is the first occasion in my professional experience when the entire cast and director fitted into one taxi." Stage fright made him irritable. "If this film unit gets any smaller, it will disappear altogether."

"Up its own orifice, you mean?" sniggered Jed.

"Not quite." But it was nearer the truth than Ivor realised.

In the hospital an anxious face peered round the door. Shirley blinked in disbelief. "Mavis?"

"Thank God for that," Mrs Bignell's prayer was heartfelt. "It's all right," she hissed to someone outside, "we've found the right place."

Shirley watched incredulously as the two she'd last seen trussed, gagged and on their way to certain doom, flopped wearily into the chairs on either side of her bed. Mr Pringle grabbed hold of the sheet for support, utterly fatigued. Even Mavis had lost her bounce.

"Are you two real?" Shirley demanded. "I told the police I was sure that man was going to kill you."

"He nearly did, dear. But Mr Pringle and I had a bit of survival training during the blitz, I think that helped. We both had the will to live, you see." Mrs Bignell clutched Shirley's hand tightly as she took in the bandaged shoulder, the drip and the haggard face against the pillow. "It was a frightening experience but I think we've been luckier than you, all things considered. How are you feeling?"

"Lousy." Shirley was puzzled. "Did the police find you? I told them what happened. Trouble was, I couldn't be sure of that man's name. You knew him though, didn't you? You recognised him?"

Mavis tried to ignore the question. She'd already rehearsed what she would tell Shirley, a version of the facts calm enough not to disturb an invalid's peace of mind.

"We were ever so lucky, dear. We were dumped but a vicar found us. We were at an oasis in one of those deserts you have out here, in a disused hotel, and this vicar happened to be passing. He and another member of his flock took us back to your ranch. We were thankful to find you weren't there, and that someone had cleared away the remains.

"When Sammy didn't arrive, we thought we'd try and find you. The hotel where we'd left our luggage . . . " She hesitated, remembering the recent unpleasantness there, "After they'd finished being rude, they suggested we try this hospital."

"Sammy wasn't at the ranch?"

Mavis saw the alarm and stroked Shirley's hand. "Now don't start worrying. We left the vicar and his friend camping at your place. They'll explain when Sammy gets home. I expect he's decided to stay the night with friends. Was it him who found you?"

"Yes."

"Well, think what a shock that must have been. Much better if someone else is looking after him, and if he does go back, those two will be there. I left some spaghetti hoops they can heat up." She lowered her voice. "We were all a bit hungry. I hope you don't mind, dear, I helped myself to what was in the cupboard."

Shirley was determined to have the truth.

"Mavis, you have to tell me. Who was that gunman? Was he something to do with the people who've rented our barn? I've been going crazy trying to work it out."

Mrs Bignell sighed. "He was Enrico Dulce, the film producer. As to why he should know your address . . . Mr Pringle and I have been worrying ourselves silly, too. None of it makes sense. We can't think what got into the man." She raised her eyes to the ceiling in search of a solution. "It must have been a brainstorm. Either that or the male menopause – I read an article – it sends some men round the bend."

"Mavis, he tried to kill us!"

"I know, dear, but Enrico's been working far too hard and that may account for it. As for what he did to the dog, I blame the violence on American television myself, and the way everyone here has a gun. I mean, you can't iron clothes with the things, can you? The only thing you can use them for is shooting people." Having delivered this homily, Mrs Bignell looked across for confirmation. To her disgust she saw Mr Pringle's head sunk against his chest.

"Wake up," she ordered. "You can't go to sleep, this is a hospital." Mr Pringle replied with a quiet, rhythmical snore. "I'm very worried about him, Shirley. He passed out on me this morning. We were tied up – the pain was shocking and *he* was unconscious – with the sun shining on his bald patch. How much would a brain scan cost, have you any idea?"

On the Strip, watched by crowds six deep outside the Beaux Rêves, Louis Carlson was locked in argument with the fire chief. As Enrico Dulce he was behaving like a caricature of a director, waving his arms, shouting, doing all that he could to distract everyone from the unit vehicles moving discreetly into position to block the street.

Ivor Henry and Monica had found a spot away from the crowds. "Shall we run through our lines?"

"Why not?" Ivor tried unsuccessfully to sound flippant. "I

don't think I've ever had a bigger audience."

"Not us," Monica pointed to the huge TV screen inside the railings. "That's what they'll be watching."

"I hope the soundman's thought of that." He was distracted, "It could interfere with our dialogue."

"They'll fix it at the dub," she comforted, "they always do."

"Why the hell isn't Pringle here to sort things out?"

"It's very odd, and I may be hearing things, but I thought I heard Enrico telling that fireman Mr Pringle was in charge."

Ivor snorted. "Thank God he's not! Where shall we start? From the top?"

Mrs Bignell was satisfied. She had persuaded a doctor to shine a torch into each of Mr Pringle's pupils and declare him to be alive, but not to depend on it. She had arranged to return to the hospital the following morning to drive Shirley back to the ranch, "although whether you'll want to travel when you see the state of our hire car, dear . . . We don't know how that happened either but I'm not going to waste time worrying about it."

Finally, she'd promised Shirley that she and Mr Pringle would see the police, confirm what had happened and tell them about Dulce.

"If you don't," Shirley said worriedly, "they may try and blame Sammy. People do, you know."

"I understand, dear. Don't fret. We'll put things right in the morning."

After that, she'd driven to a nearby motel and, mindful of the unpleasantness previously because of an unpaid bill someone had signed with the name Pringle, booked them in under Bignell.

Now, as she tucked the covers round her companion, she scowled. "This new nightie was a bloomin' waste of money." There was a TV set in the corner of the room but she no longer cared.

"Sorry Frank," she apologised, "I'd love to watch the grand finale but I'm bushed. I hate to admit it . . . it could be my age." She yawned. Ten minutes to midnight. When she'd been a girl, she could've danced the night away, but now . . . Fancy coming all this way and missing it.

Mavis Bignell pulled the duvet up disconsolately; she liked a cuddle before she went to sleep. The air-conditioning made these places awfully cold. No doubt Mrs Ellis would be scornful . . . So what? She and Mr P had reached the end of the day alive, which was more than she'd expected this morning. Mavis offered up brief thanks for deliverance and fell asleep.

Gino watched the digital seconds tick away. For the next nine minutes there was nothing more he could do. From midnight onwards, he needed to move at speed to make *his* plan work. He'd examined every point to make sure nothing could go wrong.

It was his habit to be thorough, it had kept him out of trouble . . . so far. At intervals throughout the desert, beside various power lines, his equally careful team would be in position. The leader, Al, was a man he'd worked with before.

Suddenly a helicopter buzzed low overhead. His mood changed to panic in a flash. There was no moon. Surely he couldn't be spotted! He calmed himself. What if he were? It didn't matter, not yet. Moments later the helicopter moved on and Gino steadied himself: eight minutes to go.

Outside the ballroom, a team of men was working frenziedly under orders of the facilities director. Gone was the sophisticated perfection of the décor. Panels had been unscrewed, grills flung aside, their fitments scattered, revealing ducting with its inevitable fluff and dirt. According to Detective Lieutenant Gary Hocht, the interior of each section had to be thoroughly checked.

His main problem was still unresolved, because the dangers were still unspecified. Management and sponsors had been adamant: transmission could not be interrupted.

Purcelle was with the house electrician examining the pattern on the control panels, attempting to trace any possible interference. "If only we knew what we're looking for . . . "

"We will when we see it. Keep checking."

Gary Hocht had an increasing tightness in his chest. It had to be here. The reason Judy Beeker died had to be in this building even though it eluded him. What the hell was it?

"No dice," Purcelle had forced his way through cheering crowds blocking the foyer. "We've checked every power supply, we've done spot checks on cables and so on. Nothing. Do they still refuse to clear the people out of that ballroom?"

"They do," muttered Hocht. "The sponsors don't want to

know. They're in TV control, refusing to answer their pagers."

"Where's the fire chief? Can't he use his authority? I thought he was coming over?"

"He's out on the Strip. Apparently there's a problem with some film people – "

Purcelle interrupted. "Those people waiting to go on, we could at least clear them out of harm's way . . . "

"What d'you mean?"

"The sponsors want the last few people to enter by the main door, through the audience, carrying handfuls of dollars all the way to the bowl. There's about a dozen of them surrounded by their families in the foyer. They could be asked to leave."

"Go ahead and do it." What if it did screw up the show, they'd be safe.

"Another thing, don't you think the TV people should issue a warning during the next commercial? Some of the audience might not want to get hurt. We could at least give them the choice."

"Shit, why didn't I think of that!"

"Hey!"

Covered in filth, the director from Milwaukee had emerged from a length of duct.

"This one's clean, right as far as the corner – "

"Which is the quickest way to the TV control?"

"Up the front stairs, across the hall – " But there was a further shout as Hocht began to rush away.

"Are you the guys who wanted to see me?" Two people were advancing down the hall, one of them was a detective, the other was tall, in his sixties and blind. "Someone from Homicide, they said. What the hell's it all about?" The sight of him made Hocht grind his teeth.

"This the regular piano tuner?"

"That's the one," the facilities director agreed.

"You never said he was black."

"You never asked."

More time wasted. They'd go through the formalities with the old woman for routine's sake, some other week when they weren't busy.

It took vital minutes to explain the mistake tactfully, and apologise.

As Hocht finally rushed away in the direction of TV control, he shouted over his shoulder, "Keep checking, it's got to be here some place."

"What has?" The facilities director was as frustrated as they were. "Just what the hell are we trying to find? Will someone please tell me."

"Listen," said Purcelle, reasonably "whatever it is, it's probably going to go bang in seven minutes' time and there may not be enough of us left to make a pumpkin, never mind two white mice, SO KEEP LOOKING!"

Beneath the stage, the shining bullet-proof truck was backed up with the rear doors cracked open. Metal strong boxes full of dollars were already stacked inside ready for the drive along the Strip. It was hot. Air-conditioning didn't reach this far down. There were three guards in charge of this part of the operation. Two of them grumbled as they heaved and tugged.

"They should've provided us with a few beers."

"How much longer?"

"Six minutes."

The now familiar order, this time engineered by Ozal, came out of the overhead speaker, "Stand-by to change over the box. Stand-by to change over. New box, please."

"I thought the idea was for the bowl to fill right up to the top at the finish?"

"Must've changed their minds." He nodded to the third guard, "OK, let her go," Nursing his machine gun, the man pressed the reverse talk-back button on his mike. "Standing-by," and punched in the code on the control panel.

The other two had moved to where the spare containers stood and began easing an empty one into position. The third guard stretched to ease the ache in his back.

"They should have given us a proper TV," he complained for a thousandth time, "wouldn't have interfered with security."

They heard the familiar noise as the covers closed over the golden bowl.

"That's it . . . Here she comes . . . " Simultaneously, the base panel slid aside.

In TV control, Hocht was demanding that a warning announcement be made. No one paid any attention; a row was in progress as to why the bowl had suddenly been emptied.

At the same time, below stage, a movement on the panel security screens attracted the third guard's attention. "Hey," he called jubilantly, "here comes the escort vehicle. Not long now!"

The other two slid the full container on board the security vehicle. Each was a married man with kids, they'd been selected for their integrity. As the designer had promised, not one dollar had been lost. So far.

Up in the ballroom the covers re-opened, revealing the gleaming, empty bowl. Those surrounding it were nonplussed. This wasn't what they'd been expecting. They glanced about for guidance. In the spotlight, the Star waited patiently; all he could hear over the ear-piece was chaos, exactly as Ozal had anticipated.

"What the hell's happening down there?"

"Who authorised the bowl to be emptied? I didn't!"

"Someone tell Frank to keep going!"

"What happens now?"

"We carry on as if nothing happened."

"How the hell do we do that?"

"Will someone please warn those people – " Hocht tried but was shouted down.

"We *carry on*. Someone tell Frank!"

"What the hell *has* happened, though?"

"Who gave the order – "

"Someone talk to Frank FOR CHRISSAKE!"

Below stage, the escorting police patrol car reversed towards the bullet-proof truck. The third guard let go a hand on his machine gun to wave it into position.

"Back a bit . . . straight as you are . . . back a bit more . . . "

John Millar was at the wheel; beside him, Ozal. In the rear seats, also in uniform, were the cameraman and soundman; they carried automatics.

Both rear doors swung open. The cameraman fired at point blank range into the third guard's chest then leaped into the driver's seat of the security truck.

The other two guards froze as the soundman faced them. He was tense, wondering if he could bring himself to do it; he'd never killed before but the second guard made it easy by moving a hand. The gun pumped out bullets lavishly. Hey, this was great! The guy lay on his back, completely still.

"Hurry up!" The cameraman had turned the ignition key in the security truck. The soundman jerked his gun at the remaining guard.

"On your belly." He stood astride and fired deliberately into the back of the skull. Blood and gristle spurted out of the exit wound. He was only obeying orders; Ozal had explained how necessary it was to avoid the risk of identification.

The soundman threw himself into the back of the patrol car and both vehicles moved forward. It was 23.59 and fifty seconds.

On the Strip, the fire chief had returned to his cab to consult his office about the incredible situation whereby some jerk had given permission for filming, tonight of all nights.

He stopped abruptly.

Between him and the cab there was now a four-wheel drive vehicle. Behind it, on tow and straddling the road was the make-up/wardrobe caravan. Furious, he began shouting for the driver to come and clear these new obstructions off the highway. He yelled at the rest of his team to give a hand. Men came out of the fire truck, the wardrobe mistress appeared at the door of the caravan, apparently oblivious, and blocked their passage. The fire chief began to yell.

Enrico Dulce shouted, "Roll film, end ident. Ignore what's going on, it'll add atmosphere." Monica was stunned. For one thing it looked as though the camera assistant was doing this shot, which was strange with such an important scene, and as for all the shouting in the background . . .

Enrico's voice rang out sharply. She put her worries aside and gave him her full attention. This was the scene when her character's patience finally snapped. Blanking out everything except her daughter's needs, Monica advanced to the chalk mark in the centre of the Strip. She stared at the lens, saw Enrico's nod out of the corner of her eye, and spoke her line: "I can't take any more. It's for her sake . . . for all our sakes . . . for her future . . . Don't you understand?"

Louis Carlson had raised his left hand, he could see the sweep hand on his watch: fifty-five . . . fifty-six . . . fifty-seven seconds. His voice shook, "And – cue!"

Monica whipped out the realistic toy gun. Jed Pointer moved into the right foreground frame. It was the moment he'd been waiting for, the reason he'd been cast in the part; now at last he could be as violent as he knew how.

Screaming obscenities, uncontrolled, he flew at Monica to knock the gun from her hand, and Monica fired. People began to scream on the sidewalk. Others, struggling to see, instinctively began to do the same. Louis Carlson began backing away. In a second or two, he would disappear altogether.

Inside the Beaux Rêves, the house engineer had discovered the overload on the control panel one second too late.

"That's very odd," he said.

"What is?" asked Purcelle but he was speaking into absolute darkness.

Throughout the casino, along a square half mile section of the Strip, the power failure was complete: lights went out, tills locked shut in the gambling salons, elevator doors closed, the overhead walkway stopped. Worst of all, every air-conditioning unit died.

In other casinos, stand-by generators came into operation automatically but those in the Beaux Rêves, with the cut-outs attached by Gino, tripped. It had been a perfect operation. Only one detail was missing.

Panic set in along the Strip. Out in the desert at various points along the power supply lines, the four members of Gino's team scrambled back into their cars and vanished into the night.

In the ballroom, the tight mass of bodies began to struggle. Several called for calm but as one or two, fighting for air, tried to push their way through, the first ones fell to the floor.

A stampede began. A woman keened in terror. Her husband screamed for emergency lights. Others screamed even louder: which way was the door?

Outside, only one man was able to make his way through. Unable to understand the mêlée but perfectly capable of finding an exit, the piano tuner was on his way home.

The remaining member of Ozal's team, installed by the simple expedient of paying for a ticket, had followed instructions and positioned himself below the huge chandelier. His gun which he could put together blindfold, was ready for action.

Ozal had chosen him from descriptions of his elegant silvery profile. He could have been taken for a Senator instead of the Extra he really was. He only had to perform one task but he did it well.

He fired in the direction of the ceiling. The noise, followed by a shower of glass splinters, triggered the anticipated panic: inside the ballroom, any remaining restraint disappeared in the pandemonium.

The manqué Senator allowed himself to be carried to the nearest wall by the force of the crowd. All he had to do was endure until the final act. Ozal had told him to protect himself as best he could. He crouched, arms round his head, dreaming of the five thousand dollars he would collect tomorrow morning.

Outside, the patrol car, followed by the security truck, was already beyond the empty ornamental fountains and speeding towards the exit. Below stage, the second guard in his death agony tried to reach his handset but the effort was too much.

Ahead, the automatic steel gates were stationary in a half-closed state as John Millar, swearing with shock and fright, took the only possible action: he rammed a gate, forcing it backwards, and shot through the gap. Why hadn't Louis done as he'd been ordered to? Because of his bulk, according to the plan, his task had been to force the gate open before disappearing from the area in his car. There was no time to wonder at it; with increasing speed John swept the now battered police car in a continuous screaming curve out on to the Strip.

The truck followed. Monica Moffat still stood on her chalk mark. As the vehicles swept towards her, the screech of their tyres was ear-splitting.

The patrol car swerved, juddered as the driver's door fell open, then raced away. In that split second, shock slowed everything down. A series of images printed themselves on Monica's mind's eye.

First was the driver fighting to control the wheel as he grabbed at the half-open door. Second was the man in the passenger seat. Wearing dark glasses, with teeth bared in a manic grin, it was the face she had kissed and adored all those years before. She cried his name aloud. "Ozal!"

In the fire chief's cab, an irate voice demanded to be told what was happening. Police vehicles in every part of town began switching on their sirens before discovering they couldn't communicate: someone had jammed the frequencies.

Sponsors crashed into one another as they fought to escape from the TV control room. There wasn't much point. Outside was equally dark. They shouted, demanding that all security men remain in position but no one could hear.

In front of the bank of dead screens, the TV director and his assistant sat discussing their next assignment despondently.

It was the nightmare everyone dreaded. A heist, the scoop of a lifetime, with no way of recording it. Not until power was restored.

"It could've paid for my pension," sighed the director.

"Yeah," the assistant agreed.

An anonymous voice behind them begged someone, anyone, let Frank know what was happening but no one could.

And in the communications room at the end of the hall, three minutes and seven seconds behind schedule because of a fault in the timing mechanism, the Semtex in the white plastic box taped by Judy Beeker to the cupboard wall behind the relay panels – where Detective Lieutenant Gary Hocht had failed to notice it – finally exploded.

Shock waves reached the Extra crouched low against the ballroom wall. The air was sucked out of his lungs as masonry began to bulge. Shit! Ozal hadn't told him which side of the room would be safe.

The explosion followed by the thunder of destruction, left Mrs Ellis outraged. "This never happens at home," she cried indignantly, "not even when they brought in the Poll Tax."

Mr Pringle whimpered in his nightmare. Mavis stretched out a hand across the dividing space. "Don't worry," she murmured, "Shirley's safe, it's all over. We can go and tell the police about it in the morning." And adjusting her blue-clad back with its lace inserts, she snuggled down against her pillow.

Chapter Nine

Early morning on the 18th

As night moved towards dawn, Ozal's revised plan unfolded, complete in every detail except for those actions which Gino Millar had been expected to perform. Instead, he had disappeared; Ozal didn't know why.

Why hadn't Gino been at the rendezvous with the helicopter? Was it to do with Louis? ·

Ozal had, as he'd promised, ordered Louis to go to the barn. The guy had been near breaking-point with fright but Ozal had described what would happen to his kids if he didn't obey.

There was no way any of them could contact Ozal; midnight was past, the line had been cut. Maybe Gino had had problems? The terrible alternative refused to go away: maybe Gino Millar was no longer loyal.

The radio operator had said, "I hardly recognised him, what with his hair and everything." Ozal didn't know what he was talking about; it was too late to find out.

Treachery. It festered while three guards were shot and twenty-three million dollars were driven past security cameras, along the shortest possible route before vanishing in the simplest possible way.

Treachery. Louis Carlson was too stupid to understand but Gino, clever, silent Gino knew all right.

The most savage disappointment was beside him in the patrol car: John, the one in whom he'd put his trust.

The Family had delivered their verdict: Ozal had sworn to carry it out.

The radio operator was in the removal van with the engine running. The security vehicle drove up the ramp. John and the cameraman pulled up the ramp and closed the shutters. The removal truck rolled out on to the highway; the battered patrol car, siren wailing, with the cameraman now in the driver's seat, headed back towards a certain car pound in Las Vegas.

In the removal van, John, Ozal and the soundman emptied the strong boxes, while the radio operator drove sedately towards an industrial area on the eastern side of Las Vegas.

There, a short time later, plastic sacks of dollars were transferred to a stationery supplies truck in the peace and quiet of a disused factory loading bay. The radio operator, having been paid, shot off towards Los Angeles on his roadster.

The supplies van re-emerged in the direction of the desert. The three inside now wore overalls. At the wheel, John was made nervous by Ozal's unexpected presence.

"I thought that radio guy was supposed to take you plus your share to the pick-up with Carole?"

"Change of plan," replied Ozal laconically. He didn't elaborate.

At the road block, the police officer took a cursory look at the replacement parts for a photocopier, boxes of ribbon cassettes and open sacks of shredded paper. "On your way."

John swore when he learned Ozal also intended travelling with him in the helicopter. He tried to hide fear with bluster. "What's going on?"

"You'll find out."

Ozal's own heartbeat had increased: where the hell was Gino? He daren't say he'd been expecting him. He waited to be told by someone of Gino's presence, for the sound of Gino's voice. The son-of-a-bitch wasn't here!

John had been expecting Gino, he was the one supposed to be in the helicopter. There was no time to ask if that had been changed. They'd allowed five minutes for loading and without Gino's help, he had his work cut out.

The others obeyed his instructions feverishly. Ozal listened as the soundman zipped the crew's share inside his breast pocket. The man had already wiped away memories of what his bullets had done and dreamed instead of what his share would buy: Betty wanted sables. If she was nice to him, she could have them.

His next task was to drive the stationery van across to where the power men would be waiting with his car. He didn't waste time on goodbyes. He gunned the van away into the night. Apart from Gino, the plan was moving with precision.

"Start flying," ordered Ozal. Gino would be at the barn, that was it. For some reason he didn't yet understand, Gino had had to follow a different route.

But suppose Gino *wasn't* at the barn?

For the first time since the whole operation started, Ozal began to be afraid.

Cursing silently, unaware of Ozal's tension, John put on his cans. What lay ahead was the most risky part of the operation. He listened intently to radio chatter. As soon as four police helicopters were aloft, John lifted his own machine into the darkness and began flying a pre-arranged decoy pattern, scanning highways and homesteads as if part of the search, to fool the watching radar.

No one asked him to identify himself. Christ he was lucky! There was still too much confusion on the ground. He changed his flying pattern from scanning the ground, to a much wider sweep until he reached the pencil mark on his map. Switching off his lights, flying as low as he dared, John moved sideways towards the ranch.

In the left hand seat, Ozal remained silent. John couldn't spare more than half a thought while he was flying, but he dearly wanted to know what the old man intended to do next. One thing was certain, John was safe; Ozal couldn't take over the machine!

It was amazing what a good night's sleep could do. It was still very early but that was because Mavis hadn't adjusted to the time changes and her tummy demanded food. Nothing could dampen her spirits this morning, even if a lack of items on the tray was a disappointment.

"Wake up, dear. The weather's lovely and I've found three tea-bags. It's a pity about the powdered milk but at least we can manage a cuppa."

Mr Pringle stirred experimentally, then groaned.

"What's the matter?"

"My body."

"Which bit?"

"All of it."

"Don't be silly. You must be feeling better, you snored half the night. Drink up." It was thrust under his nose. "I don't think the Americans can have heard about sugar, I can only find saccharin."

"Of course they know about it," he muttered irritably, "they realise it's bad for you, that's all." Signs of temper made her cheerful, he was obviously picking up.

"I'm in danger of losing weight. I shall have to eat lots of chocolates to make up for it. Besides, I hate the taste of sweeteners." She perched on his bed companionably. "You look dreadful. Going to do your exercises? It might help to joggle your liver." He wasn't ready to be coaxed.

"Mavis, yesterday my liver had all the joggling it needed for the next ten years. I don't feel well, which isn't surprising considering what we went through. I shall need far more than one night to get over that." She allowed him a smidgin' of sympathy.

"I know. My arms are black and blue where Enrico tied us up . . . my shoulder blades still feel dislocated." She sighed. "We'll have to find a police station after we've had breakfast and tell them about it. He could be a danger to himself until they've taken that gun off him. Listen, there's a nice big bath here. I'll fill it to the top and you can have first go, that'll help the aches. Would you like me to scrub your back?"

"It feels as if there's no skin left." But she was impatient to be on the move.

"Come on. Rise and shine. You'll feel better if you walk about. Lying in bed makes your muscles go all flabby. I'm starving. When we find a coffee shop I'm going to have some of those luscious waffles with maple syrup. Shall we watch the news? I'd love to know what the total was last night . . . I bet Frank Sinatra's feeling worn out."

Chattering, pattering across the room in her négligé and elegant blue mules with satin bows, Mrs Bignell reached for the on/off button. "I must say I always feel decadent, watching telly in a nightie, especially when the sun's shining outside . . . Oh, look, it's you!"

Mr Pringle's cup shivered against the saucer. He stared in

disbelief, all bodily discomfort forgotten. It was a photograph, taken where or when he couldn't think, of himself at a table – holding a gun!

Mavis repeated in a shocked whisper, "It is you!"

Her companion didn't utter a sound as the shot widened to include the edges of the photograph. The picture now showed part of Monica Moffat's arm plus her handbag on the table top but beyond these, in sharp focus, Mr Pringle's black and white image squinted at them as he stared along the pistol barrel.

Mrs Bignell's lips were stiff, she found it difficult to form the words. "It must've been when we were in Flagstaff . . . that first morning . . . Monica was showing us that prop gun."

"Yes . . ."

"I do wish you wouldn't wear a shirt two days running . . . look at that collar . . . "

"Shall we listen to the sound?"

With utmost reluctance, she turned it up one notch. The voice was peremptory.

"If you know this man – or think you have seen him – contact your nearest police department. We owe it to those children, to all those who donated their life savings; we have to recover every cent of that money. Twenty-three million, one thousand, one hundred and fifty-three dollars to be precise, my friends."

On screen, the shot changed to a man in a suit, glaring accusingly at the lens. In a dramatic gesture, he pointed at the two quaking figures in the motel room.

"And if *you* happen to be watching this broadcast, Pringle, don't imagine you can get away with this. The whole of America is on the lookout. The rest of the world is waiting for us to find you. And when we do: expect no mercy.

"We shall demand the ultimate penalty. And why not? You have committed the worst sin of all: you have taken the bread from starving boys and girls. You have stolen milk from a dying child. There are no words black enough to describe what you have done. To the catalogue of those infamous men in history, the list which includes Joseph Stalin and Adolph Hitler, we can now add one other name: G D PRINGLE!"

The shot changed again, to show the regular newscaster sitting alongside.

"Thank you Reverend Lamont for your message. You have

summarised the anger so many of us feel this morning. And for those of you who have just tuned in, before we give you the latest update on last night's terrible events, here is someone who wants to express in her own words how she feels. On behalf of American motherhood, ladies and gentlemen, Mrs Marilyn Schuckenhauser."

The newscaster's gaze swivelled to the incoming picture on his monitor but as the stringy blonde clutching an irate infant opened her mouth, he filled in the pause, "Take your time, Marilyn. Let us know how you *truly* feel." Mrs Schuckenhauser took another deep breath. "Let your emotion come from the heart. Imagine how it would be if it was little Jonathan there who was being deprived."

American motherhood got a word in at last: "Jacob."

"OK. Jacob."

"Yes . . . well he's a monster isn't he? I mean, the Brit. That's why, I guess. Who else but a Brit could do such a lousy thing . . . Look at Ireland. And all that money for Chrissakes! Millions and millions of dollars . . . who wouldn't want to get their hands on that! How'd he do it, that's what I want to know?"

"Marilyn, if it was *Jacob* who was being *starved*?" the newscaster interrupted urgently. "Tell us how would you feel about that?"

"Oh, Geez . . . he's a monster too, these days. Kept me up half the night bawling his head off. He's teething, I guess . . . "

The first terrifying wave had crashed over Mr Pringle's head, the ringing in his ears was beginning to subside. He came up for air and gazed wildly at Mrs Bignell, hands flapping, unable to speak.

"Aah . . . aah . . . aah . . . "

"They got your name wrong," she whispered, "it should have been G D H."

Gasping to quiet the thumping of his heart, Mr Pringle broke into speech at last. "Mavis . . . what's happened? What on earth are they saying? Last night . . . all that money? What are they talking about? Am I going mad?"

On screen, Mrs Schuckenhauser's buck teeth continued to move up and down. Jacob screamed but Mr Pringle heard nothing except the erratic thud of his life blood pushing its way along old arterial paths. His complexion sent a danger signal to Mrs Bignell.

"Here . . . don't go and have a heart attack!" she begged. "Put your head between your knees and finish your tea. I'll try and find another channel." She too couldn't believe what she'd just seen. "Maybe it was some kind of joke?"

It wasn't, but the next broadcast explained more lucidly the reason for Mr Pringle's sudden rocket to stardom.

The newscast came to an end. They watched a final repeat of Monica Moffat and Ivor Henry, both in handcuffs, followed by a sobbing Clarissa and a sullen Jed Pointer, climbing into a police van.

In a repeat of the shot, Ivor turned to camera, Adam's apple wobbling.

"We came out here to make a film . . . Pringle was supposed to be the road manager . . . He was nothing of the sort. Our producer, Enrico Dulce, has been doing all the work. You ask Pringle about all this. He knows – "

At this point, one of the officers shouted, "Move it!"

"All right, all right!" he shouted back. "Just you ask Pringle, that's all. Get him to tell you where the money is. He's been damn mean with the float as well – "

Mavis turned off the set.

"Bloody sauce! That's where they got the stupid idea. I told you Ivor once played a Nazi, didn't I? They chose the right man for the part, if you ask me."

"Mmm," Mr Pringle had begun to recover and was preoccupied.

"Fancy all that happening while you and I were asleep. I wonder if Mrs Ellis managed to see it? At least *she* won't go saying silly things to the police, she knows you too well."

"Yes . . . " He was still so blue around the mouth, he had her worried.

"Try not to get upset, shock's bad for you. I'm going to give those three tea-bags another fright but we'll have to manage without milk powder this time."

Braced with the effluent, they reviewed the situation, each trying to conceal their trembling as the enormity of their plight became increasingly apparent. Mrs Bignell began.

"Last night, when we were with Shirley, the lights went out and a bomb blew a hole in the side of the casino."

"We'd left the hospital by then. According to the report, it happened at midnight when we had already registered here."

"Perhaps that sleepy lad on the desk will remember when we checked in," Mavis said hopefully. On the other hand, perhaps he wouldn't. "Anyway," she continued, "it was pitch dark. A complete power failure."

"Over a half-mile area . . . " Mr Pringle's voice quavered as he said, "Those wretched guards . . . family men. All three of them dead . . . and I am being blamed!"

"Now don't get upset. We know it's only silly old Ivor Henry. As soon as we explain to whoever's in charge – "

"That may be difficult." Even Mavis realised that.

"Yes. Out here they seem to shoot first and ask questions afterwards. And the way they're talking, any single one of those policemen could loose off the instant he spotted you."

It wasn't a great comfort.

"That gang went to a lot of trouble," she was distracted, thinking about it. "Driving off the wrong way down the Strip in the dark. They still haven't found the security van."

"Nor the police vehicle."

"Which no one took any notice of because it was a real one, which is what they'd been expecting. I wonder if they'll ever find the money? Poor Frank Sinatra, all that effort and then for this to happen. What a good thing he wasn't killed when that wall blew apart."

Mr Pringle sighed. "The chances of finding the money by now must be extremely slim, it could be anywhere. As for that wardrobe girl . . . " He'd touched a raw nerve. Mrs Bignell was vehement.

"Giving them your photograph! How the hell did she get it, that's what I'd like to know?"

But the puzzle was falling into place; it was the same jigsaw he'd begun piecing together yesterday, on the way to Baker.

"Cutting off the power supply to such a large area required considerable forethought. A number of technically qualified people must've been involved."

Mrs Bignell stared. Why bother about them? Hadn't he understood that thanks to Ivor, these people now believed *he* was the mastermind? As if anyone who knew him could imagine he would spirit away money from deprived children! It made her blood boil! Her mood changed.

Suppose the dear old thing had lost his marbles? Damn Mrs Ellis, Mavis thought suddenly, they should never have come on this escapade. They should have gone to Bognor with the over-sixties.

Aloud, she asked again, "Have you any idea how that girl did get hold of your photograph?"

"Oh yes, that's perfectly simple. And what happened last night is the answer to everything that's been bothering me since we arrived. I knew there had to be a reason why you and I were offered a free trip to the United States."

Mrs Bignell was baffled. His colour was returning, which was a blessing, but he still looked tired. His voice grew stronger as he explained. "You and I have been used as stool-pigeons, as they say over here."

"Pardon?"

"Quite." Mr Pringle had a spurt of indignation, "It is the first – and I trust the only – time in my life when anyone has attempted to make a fool out of me. It must never happen again."

He was sitting upright, his moustache was woofly, his hair spiky, but he was full of defiance at such a hostile world. Mavis was amazed. Never mind the police force, the blood lust of Mrs Schuckenhauser and friends – was he frightened? No, he wasn't; he was magnificent.

"That's the spirit," she cried encouragingly.

Any minute the FBI could hurtle through that door. She had to let him know how she felt.

"Give us a kiss."

But Mr Pringle couldn't be distracted; the little strength he'd regained, needed to be husbanded. With infinite regret, he put her aside, asking, "Did you mention a hot bath?" Mavis understood. Another time, perhaps; if such a respite were granted. She offered succour.

"I packed a tablet of Coal Tar if you'd prefer that to lavender?"

"Thank you."

As she soaped him she said, "I don't know if you remember, last night we promised Shirley we'd collect her from the hospital – " she broke off. "Here, you don't think she will have told the police?"

Mr Pringle spread the flannel over his belly button. Warmth

percolated, quelling fractious inner tubes full of acid that threatened his equilibrium.

"She is not the sort who would be influenced by media hysteria, I think. Besides, she may not have seen any television."

Mavis said sadly, "It's in all the newspapers. They showed us the headlines."

"Ah . . . yes . . . "

It had to be faced. Mr Pringle stiffened the sinews. The blood was past summoning up but he was confident it would do what was necessary; beyond that, inessential demands would have to be deferred.

He wasn't a fool; the dangers ahead were infinite but he owed it to Mrs Bignell to maintain a brave front.

That toothy creature had cast a slur. By God, he *was* British and proud of it, despite government health warnings issued by the rest of the EEC. Nor did he intend to let Dulce and his gang get the better of him.

He stood, naked and fierce, as water gurgled down the plughole. Mavis waited with a towel. With Churchillian aplomb he stepped on to the mat and allowed her to pat various parts dry.

"We're not going to the police then?"

"I think – better not."

"So do I." She sat back, confident of his wisdom.

G D H Pringle considered: there was the matter of avoiding US forces of law and order, the female lynching party, and of convincing the authorities he didn't have twenty-three million dollars. As a former revenue man he knew instinctively that the last would prove the most difficult task.

Finally, there was Shirley Callaghan, dependent on them to drive her back to the ranch. First things first.

"I fear you will have to do the driving today as I must, of necessity, keep a low profile," he apologised, "but our priority is clear."

Helicopter pilots continued to exchange information as they skimmed above the desert. The security truck was still missing but an additional patrol car had been discovered, in a damaged condition, cheekily parked in the police compound. There was much swearing about it until certain items were found in the trunk.

The cameraman had been careless. He'd forgotten to take the police patrol uniforms to the incinerator. By the time he remembered, it was far too late to return for them. In the pocket of one was a security pass. Various forensic departments were now giving the item their full attention. Checks were also being done with aviation and car hire firms. Once every vehicle and aircraft in Las Vegas had been accounted for, the net would spread wider.

From the air, police observers directed teams towards any suspicious pattern of tracks in the sand. Other pilots continued to scan the horizon. If he were up here, the bastard couldn't stay aloft for ever.

At police headquarters, tempers were stretched; it had been such an obvious thing, the media accused, so why had it been *allowed* to happen. Buttoning tight lips, the investigation progressed, inch by inch.

None of the big boys were behind this one, their combined fury was proof: most of them had donated thousands to the appeal, they were as mad as hell, all of them eager to help. One group offered to take out the Pringle guy but the police were emphatic: they wanted the suspect brought in alive.

The police continued to let investigative journalists speculate all they wanted to about G D Pringle, it kept them off their backs. Sooner or later, when they got a better lead, they would recall them for a Press update and the whole focus might change. Sooner – or later.

The investigation into Judy Beeker's murder continued in a cooler atmosphere. The bomb had been responsible for three deaths and many injuries. However professional their attitude it was impossible for Hocht and Purcelle to remain detached now.

The wardrobe mistress had been interrogated (as Ozal intended). No connection had been discovered between her and Beeker. She had stuck to her story. Her background was checked out. She belonged to the right union, she'd worked as a freelance for various companies. She claimed to have been booked by Pringle in a phone call from England – and why not believe it? She had chits signed by him for location expenses, all the dates tallied.

She claimed the missing producer, Enrico Dulce, had been

booked in the same way. She understood he'd gone over to England to do the casting at Pringle's behest. Had she worked with Dulce before? She had not, which in the film business wasn't unusual. Did she know where he was now? She did not.

"Last I saw, he was directing the shot when the lights went out. When they came back on again, he and the crew were gone, I don't know where they went."

She answered their questions and behaved like someone who'd been badly let down. No, the crew hadn't had a generator, they'd been using available light at each location. No, she didn't know the crew's full names.

"We've been working non-stop since Thursday. There hasn't been *time* to find out." She produced her copy of the schedule. "All I dreamed about was the overtime."

Her story was unshakable because much of it was true and Ozal had coached her in the rest. Next week, with luck, she would be back working in the genuine film business, with an extra bonus tucked away where no one could find it.

There were high-level case conferences, there was a sifting of every single piece of information. As each state woke up that Sunday, people began checking motel registers. The erratic travel pattern began to emerge. G D Pringle had certainly left his trail well documented. One lone caller claimed he'd even seen the bastard in Texas.

When this filtered downstairs, Purcelle stretched tired muscles. "So what? He was a tourist, he'd got plenty of money for the fare. Why not visit Texas? Can we go look for him there?"

"Not our case," Hocht reminded. "Ours is in the morgue."

Out in the desert, regular power men worked to restore every link in the supply. Two of them knew perfectly well how last night's blackout had occurred but preferred to keep the information to themselves.

At the Beaux Rêves, once ambulances had removed the last of the injured, detectives moved in to search waist-high debris.

Somewhere, dollars were probably being fed into secret bank accounts – and they had so few leads: a blind man and his companion. And the Pringle guy, of course. How could one elderly limey drop out of sight in Nevada?

*

143

In the flat below Judy Beeker's, the old woman examined the piano tuner's picture. "He looks nice. Harmless, know what I mean? And black. Like that officer who came here."

The man from Homicide nodded resignedly. Lieutenant Hocht had warned him this was a long shot.

"Is it true what they're saying, that it was Judy who was responsible for that bomb?"

"We can't be sure, not yet." She stared at him, rheumy eyes full of pity.

"She thought the world of Scott . . . she'd have done anything if it meant seeing Scott again. Wouldn't think about the consequences."

Which was why evil men flourished, the man from Homicide thought savagely.

Monica Moffat could have been mistaken, she kept telling herself that. It was a long, long time ago. In her heart, she knew it had been Ozal in that passenger seat, but her heart didn't want to acknowledge the truth.

They were still being held after being told of their rights, but were confused as to what to do next. For a start there was no producer or road manager to make the decision. Also, the police wanted them to remain in Las Vegas until their innocence was proved.

Until telexes to the agency in the Charing Cross Road were answered, no one could prove anything. Today was Sunday, it would be several hours before that happened. None of them could remember Avril's home address or phone number.

Big Joe woke thinking he could hear the sound of a plane, flying low. He wriggled out of his sleeping bag and lifted the flap. Down the dirt track as far as the highway, nothing moved. There was no sign of life inside the ranch. What the hell, it was still too early and it was Sunday. A guy was entitled to an extra snooze.

In the hospital ward, Shirley had been helped to wash and dress. She'd had a restless night, there was too much on her mind to sleep, she wanted to get back home.

They'd given her more pain-killers but she needed to keep her mind alert. Especially after what the nurse had told her. What with yesterday and now this, Shirley's brain reeled; it was completely incredible.

The heist was perhaps, predictable. If the authorities hadn't anticipated such a thing was likely to happen, too bad. She listened with more sympathy to the list of injured brought into Casualty. Stealing was one thing, killing and maiming with a bomb was a real horror.

What gave her the shock of her life was when a certain name came into the conversation.

"This guy Pringle, he needs taking apart . . . I mean, stealing candy from kids. What sort of a bum does a thing like that?"

"Who did you say?"

"I keep telling you, it was this Brit who organised the whole damn thing. See, there's his picture." The nurse put the paper uinto Shirley's hand, "That's him. Looks real mean, doesn't he? He'd planned it with these other Brits. They came over, pretended to be making a film. Took some poor sucker of a producer for a ride, they say. He hasn't been found yet. Maybe those Brits shot him like they did the guards." Seeing Shirley's expression she said reassuringly, "Don't get upset about it. They'll catch up with him all right. Seems he was responsible for setting the whole thing up in Vegas last night, blocking the Strip while his other friends killed the guards and took off with the money. They haven't caught any of them yet but they will . . . They say the governor's really angry. He put ten thousand dollars of his own into that bowl, you know. Frank Sinatra's offered a reward, which is great. Everyone sure is sore that it's a Brit who's made a fool of us."

The nurse moved to the door and called to someone outside, "OK, you can strip the bed in here," and returned to her patient. "Is it your grandson who's coming to collect you today?"

"A . . . friend."

"Fine." Mentally, she crossed another responsibility off her list. "You can wait for him right outside in the hall. We've switched the TV on. No one wants to miss one single news item this morning!"

Shirley followed automaton-like and sat where bidden. Mr Pringle . . . and Mavis! Bloody hell! Another thought surfaced: neither would be coming to collect her after that!

She was light-headed with drugs. Could it possibly be true?

She knew very little about either of them. Next time the nurse sailed past she asked, "Has Sammy called at all? I could go home with him instead."

"I'll find out."

Common sense wavered. If Mavis and Mr Pringle really were today's Bonnie and Clyde, she'd have to find alternative transport.

Laughter was bubbling despite the horror when suddenly, an ice cold certainty hit her: the barn!

That's what it had all been about, all that mystery and paying such a high rental. Mr Kuminsky wanted somewhere to store paper, did he? Shirley Callaghan was willing to bet it could have a face value of over twenty-three million dollars.

How stupid could you get! Her old barn was the perfect place, it was so remote. That's why that gunman had been waiting for them yesterday, he must be one of the gang – but how did that link up with Mr Pringle and Mavis?

Thoughts, fears and suspicions made Shirley dizzy. There was only one way to find out. Call the police, the ones who visited her last night. They could sort out the whole damn thing. Oh, shit, Sammy.

He'd accepted money for the hire of the barn, she had paid it into the bank. Did that make them accessories? It might. How could they prove otherwise?

Forget calling the police. She had to get home fast, grab Sammy and keep clear of the place until the police had been and done whatever they had to.

"Hallo, dear. How are you feeling today?"

Shirley blinked, and blinked again. Mavis Bignell was standing there, from the flaming red hair to her dainty toes, the last person on earth she had expected to see that morning.

"Mavis!"

"Ssh . . . Have you seen the news?"

"Have I . . . ?"

"That's why I'm using a nom de convenience. Hilda Thompson."

Laughter finally exploded. Mavis wasn't offended.

"I know, it's not very original. It's my mother's maiden name. Mr Pringle said I'd better use one I could remember." Oh, great, thought Shirley.

"And what name is *he* using?" she hissed.

"Pringle," Mrs Bignell said innocently, "he's not planning to meet anyone if he can help it, you see. Have a choc."

Shirley had her hand in the bag before she realised. "You've been out shopping?"

"We had to eat," Mavis replied. "Mr P thought it better if we didn't have breakfast in a café."

"Much better!"

"I went into one of those Malls instead – "

"Maul," Shirley said automatically, "that's how they say it out here."

"Maul then. It was lovely. Open twenty-four hours, too. Now that's what I call service." Mavis munched chocolates contentedly. "We had cakes and takeaway coffee and I bought some salad for lunch."

"Mavis . . . aren't you worried?"

"Frankly, dear, I'm more annoyed than upset. I could wring Ivor Henry's neck."

"Mavis, the police believe that *your friend* is a criminal," Shirley searched for words to impress her. "The worse kind. A bastard, a killer . . . the sort you have to exterminate."

"Isn't it silly? I'd better finish these, I'm on a diet." Mavis popped the last two chocolates into her mouth and shook her head, "The very idea!"

Shirley closed her eyes. "And I believed you two could be part of a gang . . . " Mavis patted her hand.

"We all make mistakes. If you're feeling up to it, I think we ought to make a move. The car's outside."

"Fine."

"I've borrowed a wheel-chair." Thankfully, Shirley allowed herself to be transferred to it. Mavis saw her gasp.

"Here, are you sure you can manage? You're still looking very poorly."

"We have to get out of here, Mavis. I need to get to the ranch before the police find Sammy."

"Off we go, then." Cheerful, apparently unconcerned, Mrs Bignell followed the signs for the parking lot. She had the right approach, Shirley realised, behaving with justifiable innocence. As for her, she cowered in the chair, expecting to be challenged at every corner. Once outside, she asked, "OK, so where have you hidden him? It must be somewhere smart, his picture's everywhere and the only person who isn't out looking for him this morning is the President of the United States."

"Mr P's not in hiding," Mavis was piqued. "He's not one to run at the first sign of trouble, you know. We talked it over and decided the best thing would be a disguise."

"A what?"

"It was his idea," she said proudly. "There you are, over there in the back of the car. Now who would recognise him looking like that?"

Shirley fought back hysteria. In the damaged limousine sat Mr Pringle, wearing identical clothes to those in the photograph. Even the panama hat was in place. The only difference she could see was a piece of white lint over one eye.

"I did the bandage," Mavis told her.

g   Shirley wanted to cry.

"Mavis, I've seen the shot of him wearing those things a dozen times in the last half hour – "

"No you haven't. That's a clean shirt."

"Mavis, he sticks out like a sore thumb. People over here don't wear sports jackets and Fair Isle pullovers, they wear jeans."

"Oh, you wouldn't get him into those," Mrs Bignell was adamant, "not Mr P. He's always worn grey flannels. Those are his best ones, he keeps them for holidays. I wouldn't ask him to change the habits of a lifetime. He's finding it difficult enough as it is, you wouldn't want him to be *uncomfortable* as well?"

Shirley acknowledged defeat. They must have had the devil's own luck so far.

"We'd better get away fast," she repeated. "Any minute now they'll find out the number of that hire car and broadcast it."

"We thought of that." Mavis pushed the chair across. "Most people don't look at us or the plates. They point at the damage when we go past."

Which wasn't surprising, thought Shirley.

"We still don't know how that great dent in the wing happened."

Shirley said tiredly, "You left the keys in it?"

"Well, yes . . . " Sammy, obviously.

Mr Pringle raised his hat courteously as she maneouvred her way in.

"Forgive me for not assisting you. I am keeping what is known as a low profile."

"I'm glad to hear it." The pain was acute as she tried to lean against the seat. "Before we start, I have to tell you something; I think I know what's been going on. The men who hired the barn could be the bunch who robbed the Beaux Rêves last night."

"Ah-hah!" Mr Pringle nodded with approval, "Great minds think alike!"

"Your Enrico Dulce's mixed up in it, otherwise it doesn't make sense."

"My sentiments entirely," Mr Pringle agreed again.

"So . . . we could discover him and his friends dividing last night's haul in my old barn . . . and before we do . . . Well, I think we should at least talk about it."

Mr Pringle beamed. "You and I have reached precisely the same conclusion."

Aren't you worried, Shirley wanted to yell, aren't you scared of meeting all those . . . those killers? But Mavis was staring at her partner accusingly.

"You never told me any of that."

"I didn't want to alarm you further," he replied. She looked at Shirley.

"Aren't you bothered about Sammy?"

"Frantic! If only he's got the sense to stay out of trouble – "

"There is another little problem at the ranch at present," Mavis interrupted, "or rather, there's two."

"What?"

"Yes, our rescuers," Mr Pringle sighed, "they may be in for an unpleasant surprise. I regret to say they are particularly noticeable and therefore vulnerable."

"The vicar?"

"Irwin's more of a prophet than C of E," said Mavis, "but it's their lorry that's the problem. It's got this red-headed whore painted on the side. You can't miss it."

"We'll have to go to the police, it's the only way . . . " Shirley was fatalistic but Mr Pringle coughed, delicately.

"Mrs Bignell and I would rather not, if you don't mind. From what we've read of American justice, at the very least it could delay our return home for many weeks."

"He's told them when to start delivering *The Guardian* again you see, that's the problem," Mrs Bignell explained. "And another thing: we saw a programme about the way you execute people over here. Injecting them, giving them cyanide to sniff or frying them in that chair – some of them perfectly innocent black people. We decided we'd rather be on our way before any more mistakes were made. After we've found the money and handed it over, of course. Otherwise, they could go on believing it really was Mr P's fault."

Shirley's eyebrows rose until they could go no higher.

"How the heck d'you plan to manage that?"

Mr Pringle brushed a hand over his moustache. "With your permission, I have devised a possible modus operandi."

"A what?" she asked bluntly. He began to explain.

It had taken Louis Carlson all night to drive out to the far side of the outcrop behind the barn and climb to the top. He'd followed part of Ozal's instructions – he'd been too shit scared for his kids' survival to do otherwise – and he'd arrived at the designated spot, but by a different route. What the hell, it could be a trap! And it was uncanny that Ozal should suggest the barn after what had taken place here.

Louis's original pay-out was to have been made back on West 46th, in that same dingy office. He'd liked that idea, it appealed to the latent actor in him. He'd planned to arrive in a beat-up truck as if he was collecting garbage.

Now, spread-eagled on sun-baked rocks, he watched through binoculars. According to Ozal, he should have been down there inside that barn, ready to collect his share. There was no sign of anyone to give it to him. Apart from a few beasts grazing, there was no sign of life at all.

The sun wasn't too high, it had just gone eight. He hoped to God he could get through this business and be back at his car before it was. He was out of condition, the climb had been bad enough but stuck up here, the heat could finish him.

Louis couldn't see where the helicopter had gone. It had flown in low, he'd had to slide back out of sight and in doing so had wrenched his ankle. He was a New York boy, you didn't have rocky outcrops in New York.

He hated being here. The sight of the ranch even at this distance made his gorge rise. "I had to do it . . . I just had to, Beth." But she wasn't speaking to him. Neither she nor her mother answered the phone any more, neither did Ozal.

Last night, after Louis had been given his new orders and had escaped from the Strip during the confusion, he'd tried to call Ozal. He'd lost his nerve, he wanted so much to be a part of the Family again. He wasn't a loner. Hell, who was he trying to kid? He hadn't the guts, he needed to be part of a team.

Ozal would understand. He alone had the power to grant expiation but he wasn't available. It had happened exactly as he'd promised: after midnight, that special number registered as unobtainable. There was no way now that Louis could contact him.

After that, Louis decided he'd have to follow what was left of his own plan. It wasn't much but he couldn't think of anything better.

After the business with the dog, he'd thought of a new scenario. It was taken from an old script. Only problem was, it depended on everyone behaving as per the storyline.

According to that, Louis would have confronted Ozal with Monica. He'd even learned the lines so he wouldn't mess it up! He would have given Ozal the choice: Monica's silence to his wife about their illegitimate child in exchange for Ozal's share of the heist. Ozal always boasted how good his marriage was, he'd have capitulated. As for Monica, Louis would have been generous. She could have travelled home first class. How many bit-part actresses could boast of that?

In the most daring move of all (but it had worked for Humphrey Bogart), Louis would have been inside the barn when John and Gino arrived. He'd even planned how to spring out and surprise them into handing over their shares, like an Omar Shariff character. But he'd screwed that up by arriving too late. He'd no idea if it was the right helicopter. Suppose it was the police! He daren't make a move until he was certain.

If the scenario had been as *he'd* planned it, by now he would have been rendezvousing with Beth. It would have been so romantic! Once he opened the trunk and she saw twenty-three million dollars, Louis Carlson would have been . . . irresistible!

With the kids they would have flown into the sunset, or rather San Paulo. There they could have lived like lotus-eaters for ever.

Now he was going crazy because the sun was burning the back of his neck.

Christ, what a mess!

He couldn't crawl back empty-handed, Beth wouldn't open the door. His only chance was to grab what he could, and disappear fast.

He might have to kill whoever was in that helicopter. The idea made him sick; suppose it were John and Gino? He'd have no scruple about John but his best friend – he couldn't do it! Louis's face was wet. He was back at the same unacceptable conclusion: to double cross meant killing people. Either that or be killed himself.

If this really was a trap, he could disappear off the planet and his kids would never know. He had done as Ozal asked and destroyed all traces. An unidentified corpse in Nevada would never be connected to Louis Carlson, New York bum!

If only Beth would answer the phone!

Just where the hell was that helicopter? By the time Louis had climbed back up high enough to see, it had vanished.

If it were beyond the barn, when the sun rose higher he ought to be able to make out the shadow. Louis focused his binoculars on the distant truck with its weird markings. What was that doing here? Surely Gino's team hadn't turned up already, in a thing like that?

God, it was hot! He hadn't thought to bring any water. In New York, you wanted a drink, you stepped into the nearest bar. Was he going to die of sun-stroke up here?

Chapter Ten

"Captain, the Moffat woman says she can't sleep until she's told you about what she *thinks* she saw on the Strip. She keeps saying she's not entirely *sure* about it but it's troubling her so much she thinks she ought to tell someone."

The captain shuffled the sense out of it. He hadn't slept either, not since the night before last, and it would be a long time yet before he saw his bed. He finished his tenth cup of coffee, which for his health's sake was a de-caff. "OK, let's go listen to the lady. Where's Hocht?"

"He and Purcelle are on their way."

The captain rose and stared accusingly at the TV, still switched on in the corner of his office. In the film company's caravan, more photographs had been discovered and passed to the media. As a result he was now watching a shot of the unknown Mrs Mavis Bignell, also missing. Hand on hip, the other waving a pistol, the expression on her face was that of one who has just shouted "Olé!"

"Look at that . . . who in Fred Karno does she think she is?" he demanded heavily.

"A gangster's moll?"

"Turn the damn thing off. It makes me feel such a horse's ass just to see her!"

In the interview room, Monica sat facing the three men. Another officer stood by the door. In a corner, a girl tapped away, recording their conversation. It was like every law series she'd ever watched except this time it was real. If ever she got the chance to play such a part, she must cannibalise on this feeling.

Oh, God! Stop thinking like that. It was people's lives, her own . . .

"I know Ivor believes Mr Pringle is in some way responsible for what happened. I'm sure he's wrong. He didn't know Mr Pringle as well as I did. I've had more time to chat to him and Mrs Bignell." This had been said in her earlier statement; the captain shifted impatiently.

"Thank you for your opinion, Miss Moffat. We're checking everything out." They waited for her to continue, the silence was unnerving.

"I think I know the man who was sitting in the passenger seat of the police patrol car."

"Uh-huh." This was what mattered. The stares were so intent Monica found herself reddening.

"I was standing in the middle of the road. As the patrol car crashed through the gate in that great swerve, the driver's door fell open and the lights flickered on inside. It was only for a second or two before the driver pulled it shut but I caught a glimpse of them."

"OK, Miss Moffat, who d'you think you saw?"

"The driver was a stranger, I'd never seen him before. Late twenties at a guess, I really didn't notice. It was the other man . . . I knew him years ago. At least, I think it was him."

"A long time ago, Miss Moffat?" asked Hocht.

"Yes." She swallowed. "I was appearing on Broadway. It didn't have a long run. He was young, we both were. He was a rising star among the producers of those days even though he was still learning the ropes. Sound, lighting, that kind of thing. He was very keen on sound techniques." She paused, still stalling.

"And his name, Miss Moffat?"

"John O Halling. Not O apostrophe, he used to get bored explaining he wasn't Irish. He had a Turkish grandfather, the O was for Ozal. He preferred to use that."

"And you're sure, after . . . how many years?"

"Nearly thirty." She was bright red now.

"Thirty years is a long time, Miss Moffat."

"We were lovers . . . there was a reason we were unable to . . . " But she couldn't bring herself to talk about that. "I loved him very dearly . . . " She couldn't meet their eyes, she was so embarrassed. For them, it was an objective assessment.

154

The guy had probably been married, that kind of thing mattered in those days. But was this woman reliable? It was a hell of a long time, had shock heightened her imagination? Gary Hocht shifted restlessly.

The captain probed, "So . . . you reckon you wouldn't mistake John O Halling, even now." Monica gave a choky laugh.

"I doubt it. I read about his accident, there was an account in *The Stage*. I found the old feeling building up inside. You know how it is." Her look implored him not to laugh. The captain didn't, he nodded seriously.

"I know. Whoever else . . . it's still there, one little part that always belongs to a certain person. You said accident?"

"Yes. The article implied Ozal was recovering from his injuries. He'd left the business by then. I'd no idea he'd since gone blind."

One of the men opposite was suddenly very still. "You're sure about that, Miss Moffat?" She was tense, forcing herself to run through every tiny detail of those images.

"No, I'm not . . . it was an impression. I knew the accident had left him with facial injuries. I think I glimpsed a scar. He had on dark glasses. But in that patrol car – it was such a swerve and he wasn't looking where they were going. His head was sort of, tilted in the wrong direction, not staring through the windscreen. Even when the driver grabbed at the door. Anyone who was a driver . . . you wouldn't take your eyes off the road in that situation, would you?"

The tall, lanky lieutenant was on his feet and heading towards the door, calling his thanks, followed by the sergeant. Monica was startled. The captain put out a sympathetic hand.

"Listen, that was good observation, Miss Moffat. We may have to ask you to check out a few photographs. D'you think you could do that?"

"Of Ozal?"

"From our records," he said carefully. "Up to you to say if they remind you of anyone. One other thing. Did this Mr John Ozal Halling have any particular male friends when you knew him? A much younger man? A man like the one driving the car last night."

"It was we who were young," her voice was quiet. "I didn't notice anyone else in the world that summer. I'm certain I've never seen the other man before."

Outside, Purcelle protested, "Listen, she could be mistaken . . . all that time ago. And maybe she came to the States *expecting* to see the guy again."

Hocht's face was impassive. "It's worth checking to see if she did, though."

Gino waited in the empty stationery supplies truck. His own car was a distance away, under more of the camouflage netting. It had been hired under the name Kuminsky, now it contained a body in the trunk. The soundman who'd driven it to this remote location had assumed incorrectly that Gino was one of the power gang, come to collect it a little early.

It had been a terrible risk. Helicopters and spotter aircraft were chasing all over the sky now it was daylight. The truck was in the shelter of a band of scrub but once the sun rose higher, it would be clearly visible. As for the car, he hoped it wouldn't be spotted for a few more hours.

Gino had assessed the risk of including the man in, but he was one of Ozal's trusted lieutenants. After exchanging a sentence or two, the man settled it by threatening to phone the Family in Los Angeles.

As he'd cleaned his knife in the sand, Gino knew from now on he was committed: John, Ozal and finally, Louis. He hoped that would be an end of it. There would be bad dreams, there always were, but Myra would help him through it.

"Come on," he whispered to the empty desert, "don't keep me waiting. We got lots to do today."

He wasn't sure from which direction they would come, he guessed in a circuitous route from Las Vegas. This morning, two power men would show up for their normal maintenance shift, as they'd be expected to after hearing the news. The other pair, the ones scheduled to drive this van to the barn, included the team leader, Al, which was important. Gino needed a man whom he could trust. He began to consider what size of bribe he would offer as a reward.

The second man was more of an unknown quantity. What was to happen to him? Gino hadn't decided yet. He would play it cool, watch Al's attitude, make the decision when the time came. It might need three of them up at the barn. The time to decide was afterwards.

"Come on, come on!"

Ozal's plan had specified nine o'clock. They needed to drive fast and be at the barn while the helicopter was still on the ground. He had left John and Ozal in the lurch, they would have to repack the dollars themselves and this would slow them down but not by much. He didn't think Ozal would be so crazy as to kill John there.

The method of packing wouldn't have changed either, Gino was certain. The empty cartons were ready in the barn and they couldn't go on using garbage bags topped with trashed, shredded paper.

High inside the rafters, Sammy had watched the dawn develop. First there had been the helicopter arriving while it was still dark. It had come from a different direction this time but still clung to the contours of the hills and landed much closer to the barn. Sammy had wished he'd had his binoculars but he daren't go and fetch them now. He peered out into the soft pink light.

Two figures had emerged. He had been sure one was Mr Freeman, which had made his heart beat so loud, Sammy could scarcely breathe.

Had he come for his car? Those strangers had taken it, the red-headed lady and the old-fashioned man. There was only the pick-up and that still had no gas; besides, Mr Freeman wouldn't want to use that. In his eyrie, Sammy had prayed to be spared from Del Freeman's wrath.

When he'd opened his eyes, he'd been astonished. The helicopter was half-way into the barn. The two men were sliding it inside, their heads ducked to avoid the drooping rotor blades. As he'd watched, the barn doors were pulled shut. The landscape was empty, there was nothing to be seen.

Then he'd noticed the tent flap beside the truck begin to twitch but no one had emerged. After a minute or two it had been quiet again. The two men must have been asleep.

As the sun rose higher, Sammy's conscience began to ache. He could hear the beasts lowing and knew they needed water. He hadn't checked the trough. Grandma would scold him. Grandma was in hospital with mysterious machinery connected to her body. Sammy stuffed his knuckles in his mouth. His ma and pa had died in that hospital after the accident. He'd been taken to see

them, they'd been as white as Grandma was now. If she died –
and Mr Freeman remained in the barn – he might have to stay up
here for ever!

Inside the barn, John had taken charge but Ozal had worked just
as fast. He'd waited in vain for John to exclaim that Gino was here
and that Louis Carlson's body was lying on the floor but John had
remained silent. Ozal had faced the unpalatable truth: Gino was
as treacherous as the rest.

After the first six cartons were packed and taped securely, John
drawled, "OK, Ozal, suppose you tell me what's going on?"

"Later," Ozal was curt. "We haven't time." He flicked open
the braille watch and touched the face, "At this rate, it'll take a full
half-hour, I'd allowed twenty minutes. Give me another box."

John handed it over and tore off a length of tape. Now they
were safely down he could think things out. Ozal still hadn't told
him why they'd needed to hide the chopper instead of leaving it
outside, ready for immediate take-off.

There were far too many unanswered questions. Why the
change of plan now? When they'd had the row about Judy
Beeker, Ozal had said nothing. Why had Louis not done what he
was supposed to, back on the Strip? Jesus, that had been a bad
moment, seeing those great iron gates half-closed instead of
Louis's bulk forcing one of them open. And where the hell was
Gino?

It had been a complete balls-up. The Family needed someone
strong, that was obvious. After this, John was going to be boss, if
only to protect his own neck. Once those dollar bills were safely
on board he could take off and leave Ozal's body right here. Why
not? In Nevada John Millar was Del Freeman, there wouldn't be
any risk.

But before that could happen, he had to know what was going
on.

"Listen, Ozal, quit stalling – "

"Are the grey cartons ready?"

"Sure . . . " As if he'd let those power men have their pay-out;
he was going to keep the lot.

"Now we start packing the rest." Ozal clicked his fingers,
"C'm on, kid, don't keep an old man waiting."

Sulkily, John kicked another box across.

Ozal could tell a lot from those small explosions of sound. Distances for instance. Sound bounced off hard surfaces and he'd learned to read pitch and echo. He had listened to every move John had made since they came into the barn. He knew which side the empty boxes were, where John was stacking the full ones over by the door.

They had kept to this end of the barn. Beyond the chopper, there were obstacles; old, rusting machinery, bales of wire and fencing posts. Gino had described the place well at the briefing in New York. Gino must be on his way here, or outside. Maybe he'd already hidden Louis's body? That was it; he'd be out there, waiting and watching to see what happened. Ozal had told him he would deal with John, and so he would. He wouldn't keep Gino waiting a moment longer than necessary. Confidence was returning by the minute; of course Gino was trustworthy. He could drive him to where Carole was waiting before heading off to join Myra. It was going to be as smooth as silk!

"What's the time now?" he asked.

"Ten after. Those men aren't due here till nine o'clock. Hey, you still haven't said: where the hell did Gino get to?"

"When we've finished." Ozal snapped the fingers of his left hand this time. "Don't stop. Give me another box."

"Pity you can't see the money," John said carelessly, "millions and millions of dollars . . . gives a man a real flip."

He was assessing whether he could push the helicopter outside unaided, and decided he couldn't. It would take for ever. So would reloading. Hell, they really had to work if he were to be ready for take-off before those other bums arrived, because he'd overlooked the need for extra fuel.

It would only take seconds to shoot Ozal but John needed to get the chopper refuelled and have Ozal help him slide it clear of the doors before he could do that.

Carrying a heavier passenger, plus additional decoy flying, had thrown John's calculations. He'd left two cans here on that previous visit, as a precaution. To make it easier, he stopped packing now and dragged them nearer the machine. Even using both, the tank would be less than two-thirds full, which cut down his range. He'd worked out alternative flight plans, naturally, but which should he use?

He began running through them, whistling through his teeth.

It was a habit Ozal knew well; it meant John Millar was no longer concentrating. The next time he leaned forward and began taping a box . . .

Ozal sprang from a crouched position, hands outstretched and took John by the throat, crashing him down on to his back.

"Jeez-sus!"

With all the power of his body Ozal was pushing John down and using his legs to clamp him to the floor. He daren't let him roll from under.

There was a split second when John might have survived, if he hadn't felt contempt and disbelief at what was happening.

It was long enough; it gave Ozal sufficient time to pinion John's arm with an elbow. That, and the heavy reel of tape encumbering John's other hand, turned the balance.

John struggled, banging the reel against Ozal's head, shoulders, anything within reach. The dark glasses disintegrated revealing scars and the empty, ugly eye-sockets.

He tugged at Ozal's head to try and pull him down; Ozal jerked backwards, still throttling, squeezing tighter, tighter . . . John tried to pull away, to bite, to wriggle his body from beneath but Ozal was solid and immovable. John's eyes were bulging now, his skin was mottled. He flailed and managed to slice Ozal's face with the edge of the reel. He pounded the place again and again until the blood poured down, saturating his own wide-open mouth with its bitter taste.

He couldn't believe Ozal was succeeding. It wasn't possible! He was younger, fitter, more intelligent. If he could reach his gun . . . only one hand . . . either hand . . . he could fire from the hip, through the stomach. Anything to stop the relentless choking pressure. John could no longer see . . . His teeth clenched in an involuntary spasm, biting through his rigid tongue.

Ozal didn't let up for a full five minutes longer than was necessary, as a precaution.

It was done. Adrenalin surged through him. He rose, brushing away unseen dust. Victory was sweet, the age-old battle of the king seeing off the young usurper. It was good to feel so strong!

There was a noise, some kind of car was headed this way – it must be Gino. In a moment he would discover what had happened to Louis. They would stack the cartons inside and drive like hell. From now on, Gino would be his eyes, his successor.

Full of purpose, throwing caution aside, Ozal headed towards the door. "Gino – "

They were surprisingly buoyant, determined to keep up one another's spirits. Not that there was anything to be cheerful about. In Shirley's opinion, Mr Pringle's "course of action" wouldn't improve anyone's life expectancy. It involved a cautious approach to the ranch, then a three-point turn so that the limo was ready for a swift getaway. Shirley was adjured to keep her eyes peeled and shout at the least sign of anything suspicious, to give Mrs Bignell every chance. It wasn't a role with much risk, she couldn't complain.

Mr Pringle's hope, that if Sammy appeared they could haul him on board and escape, was optimistic. Even more so was his suggestion, if the gang were in the barn, to let down the tyres of their getaway vehicle, then despatch Sammy to summon the police.

"If we remain hidden and take notes of their appearance, we could at least furnish a comprehensive description should the gang escape. It will assist with my efforts to clear the slur against my name. Also, as a reward has been offered, by handing over the money ourselves, you can claim it." He beamed at Shirley happily, "It will enable you to clear your overdraft. Let us hope it all comes to pass."

Shirley bit back any sarcasm. The two of them were doing their best. All she hoped for was to find Sammy and clear out.

They saw the sign for the drive-in coffee shop ahead. Shirley had just finished explaining what it meant when Mavis impulsively wrenched the wheel, turning the limo off the highway to join the queue.

"What are you doing?"

"Listen, dear, we didn't have a proper breakfast back in Boulder City, and you're looking very peaky. We need to keep up our strength at our age. This is exactly the sort of place where they don't take notice of the customers. Now, what's the American for six doughnuts and three coffees?"

Mr Pringle adopted an even lower profile as the paper bags were thrust at them. Mavis paid and sat, waiting expectantly.

"Drive on," hissed Shirley. "What's the problem?"

"He hasn't said, 'Have a nice day.'"

"Maybe he doesn't feel like saying it, get going will you!" Mavis leaned out towards the service window.

"Ta, very much, dear," she said loudly. "Toodle pip." Shirley rolled her eyes heavenwards. "Don't fret," Mavis was carefree. "He won't understand, he probably thinks I'm Japanese."

"With red hair?"

"Let me know when you see a lay-by. It's silly to try and eat while I'm driving, it could give me indigestion."

Revived and slightly overwrought, Mavis slowed the limo as they approached the familiar yellow marker indicating the turn-in to the ranch. Unbidden, she broke the tension with her wobbly soprano.

"Do not forsake me, oh, my dar-ling . . . "

"No hymn-singing now, Mavis, please!"

"It's not a hymn," Shirley told him grimly. "It's *High Noon*. You're being a bit previous, Mavis. It's only five to nine."

Mrs Bignell pulled the wheel too sharply and caught the corner post.

"Careful!"

"What the hell, it's not our car."

Mr Pringle moaned. About seven hundred pounds for renewing the bodywork . . . goodness knows how much for the front bumper. One new halogen headlight. He tried to remember the terms of contract he'd signed such a short time ago as Mavis lurched into a pothole and came up against solid rock. "Geronimo!" she cried. "We can shred the tyres to pieces as well if we want, it doesn't matter."

"I thought the idea was to arrive with a certain amount of caution?" said Shirley, breathlessly.

"It was," cried Mr Pringle.

"I *know*." Mavis bumped along, increasing speed with every yard and oversteering vigorously. "We'd forgotten how bright the daylight would be. Anyone looking out must have seen us by now . . . all we can do is . . . zig-zag so they can't hit us if they start shooting . . . and act fast before I lose my nerve! Hallo?" The limo came to an abrupt halt alongside the verandah. "Have those two left already?"

Mr Pringle saw the folded tent and pile of camping equipment.

"I don't think they can have gone far."

It was so quiet it seemed foolish to behave like the terrified soul he was and stay inside the car. Mavis was already out. Between them they helped Shirley up the steps into her chair.

"I'll fetch some water. You'd better take one of your pain-killers."

"Watch out . . . for any gunmen," Shirley gasped. Mavis banged the fly-screen defiantly.

"Anyone home?" she shouted. "There're hundreds of us so come out with your hands up, please." Mr Pringle waited, his heart in his mouth. Nothing. "It's all right, there's no one here . . . " She marched inside and he heard water being poured. On his own, he went for a cautious prowl round the back of the ranch. When he returned, he waited until Shirley had swallowed her pills and the taut face had relaxed a little.

"It's true, there doesn't seem to be anyone. Our two rescuers appear to be exploring. Their lorry is parked outside the barn. There's no sign – " He broke off. "That sounded like someone calling your name?"

"Grandma, Grandma!" Shirley turned. Sammy was careering towards them. "Come and see what's happened! It's Mr Free-man, Grandma. He's in the barn and he's dead!"

"Dead!" Mr Pringle no longer felt brave.

"Calm down, love, calm down." Sammy stopped, frightened by the sight of her face.

"You're not going to die, Grandma?"

"No, love. Not yet, anyway. Now, tell us what's happened. Slowly."

He told them about the helicopter, the long wait before Big Joe and Irwin emerged from their tent and how they had poked around the house before driving up the old track to explore some more.

"They was having a good look at everythin'. The one with the hat went in the barn. He come out, yelling. Then the little one went in. He threw up when he come out. I could see they ain't got guns so I come down and went to take a look. Mr Freeman's lying dead with his tongue hanging out, Grandma. An' there's another man dead, too. His head's half cut off."

"Oh, good heavens!" The familiar queasiness had returned. Mr Pringle could read Mavis's mind as they stared at one another: was the second man Enrico Dulce? He prayed devoutly that it wasn't. Dastardly though Dulce's behaviour had been, it didn't merit that retribution.

"I remembered to fill the trough, Grandma. An' I fed the stock. Then I see'd you coming and I ran back."

"Good boy, Sammy."

Sammy was gazing at Mrs Bignell.

"That your picture drivin' them high steppin' horses on that truck?"

"Sadly, no," said Mavis. "That is one of Enoch's assistants, I believe." She was waiting for Mr Pringle to act. He cleared his throat.

"I think it would be advisable . . . if I were to ascertain – "

"I'm coming with you," she said quickly. "Sammy, you stay here and look after your grandma."

"Whatever you do, take care," begged Shirley.

Mavis drove up to the barn much more cautiously. Ahead they could see the white canvas shape of the lorry. Big Joe was on the ground, propped against a wheel. The prophet of Enoch crouched beside him. He looked ready to run until he recognised them.

"We had nothing to do with it! I swear by Almighty God – "

"Don't bother with all that," Mr Pringle said tiredly. "Save it for the police. It is true, then? And are both men dead?"

"The big fella's throat's sliced through. The other looks as if he's been strangled."

Mr Pringle tried to pretend it was happening to someone else. Straightening his shoulders and with Mrs Bignell clutching his arm, he walked steadily towards the barn.

"I wouldn't go inside if I was you, Miz Bignell," called Big Joe. "It ain't nice in there."

Mavis's grasp tightened. "We have to look, don't we, dear. We need to be sure if either of them is Enrico."

She closed her eyes as she entered. Mr Pringle stopped and she opened them again. On his side beneath the helicopter lay a stranger, one foot still trapped beneath an overturned container of aviation fuel. It looked as though he'd run full tilt, tripped and put out both arms to break his fall – but far, far too low. How had he missed seeing that deadly shining metal rotor blade? It had severed through the soft tissues of his throat. One outflung arm, hand clenched in the dirt, was saturated with blood. Then she saw the empty socket and understood.

"He must've been blind," she whispered.

"He tripped over that container by the look of it . . . Oh, dear me!" Mr Pringle was finding it difficult to breathe. His glasses had misted over. There was a dull brown patch on the metal surface.

"Poor soul, all that blood! It looks as if he was struggling to get up again . . . What a dreadful way to die!"

"You stay here. I'll take a look at the other one."

He moved unsteadily, a little further inside.

"This isn't Dulce, either," he called. "We haven't seen him before."

"Is he dead?"

"Oh, yes." Very. "Wait for me in the car." Averting his gaze from the half-bitten tongue, Mr Pringle took several deep breaths before noticing the sacks of dollars, surrounded by cartons.

It took a moment to realise, and then his emotions were mixed. Satisfaction at having deduced correctly was as nothing now he'd seen the consequences. He heard a movement and turning, found Irwin staring at him from the doorway. Beside him, Mavis hovered.

"You realise what this money is, of course?"

"Manna from Heaven," suggested the prophet defiantly.

"Balderdash! It's the results of last night's appeal and you damn well know it. How much have you filched?"

"Ain't touched a thing, darn it!" Irwin clenched his fists. "I was busy tendin' Big Joe."

"Then we must hurry. We need to be away from here before the rest of them arrive."

"Rest of who?"

"Mr Dulce for a start," said Mavis. "The one who dumped us in Death Valley? He's part of an enormous gang and they've all got guns." She indicated the corpses. "This is what happens when he's crossed."

"Almighty God!" Irwin was torn between greed and the desire to survive. Mr Pringle issued his orders calmly.

"We'll need to use your lorry. Empty it so that we can stack these cartons in the back."

"That's more like it!" Irwin dashed outside and hauled his partner to his feet. "C'm on Big Joe. There's a posse headed this way, we got to get moving."

With tremendous zeal he began unloading his personal effects.

Mr Pringle spoke quietly to Mavis. "It's extremely dangerous. Dulce may indeed arrive and we have no way of contacting the police. The risk is considerable but if you're agreeable I think we should try and hand the money over ourselves. That way, Shirley would be entitled to the reward."

"Can't we leave it here and tell the police where to find it?"

"By then Dulce may have taken it, Irwin and Joe absconded with it, or the police seek to claim the success for themselves. I don't think Shirley would benefit in any way. I must admit my first instinct was to flee. However, if we do, you and I will remain objects of suspicion, liable to arrest. Viewed in that light, I don't think we have much choice, do you?"

"No," she said bravely "So what happens next?"

"There's less chance of our being stopped in Irwin's lorry. No one flags down a Moonie and asks for a lift, do they? Go and warn Shirley, she'll have to come with us because of the danger. And bring Sammy back here. He's a strong healthy lad when it comes to stacking boxes."

"Right!"

There were rolls of tarpaulin in the barn. Mr Pringle spread one over John Millar, the other over Ozal. He fetched a rusty wheelbarrow, loaded it and took the first batch of cartons outside.

Irwin crowed at the sight, "Money-money-money-money-money! Makes the world go round!"

Shirley was adamant. She waved jeans and an old checked shirt at Mr Pringle.

"These were Cal's. Put them on."

"Shirley!"

"I'm not leaving here with you looking like that. Anyone might recognise you and pull a gun."

"That is precisely the situation I'm attempting to avoid – "

"I mean a bystander, wanting his moment of glory."

"Good Heavens!"

"It could happen, especially after all that business on TV, so put them on. And this old hat."

Mavis packed his sports coat and flannels in the suitcase.

"You do look different," she encouraged.

"No doubt," he said stiffly. "Shall we go?"

The prophet was sulky when the last of his passengers squashed in beside him; Mavis, Shirley and Mr Pringle were in front, Big Joe and Sammy sat in the back, legs dangling over the tailboard.

"I don't need you all," Irwin whined. "Me and Big Joe can deliver the dough ourselves."

"You probably could but you may have sticky fingers."

"Pardon me?"

Mavis sighed. This language problem really was a nuisance.

"Have any dollars transferred themselves into your pockets?"

"No!"

"You sure?"

"You calling me a liar?" demanded Irwin. From where he sat Mr Pringle reached out and lifted the leather stetson. Balanced on Irwin's pate, was a stack of notes.

"May God forgive you. And Enoch as well," Mrs Bignell said piously. "Now, drive carefully. Shirley's arm is still very painful."

Irwin had a wild idea of ditching his human load and driving like hell for the Mexican border but with one cylinder not firing and no second gear, Jesus wept! He thumped the wheel with frustration.

They had driven a few miles when Shirley said suddenly, "The van coming towards us – keep going! Don't stare! Someone try and read what's on the side."

"What's up?"

"It's heading in the direction of our ranch. See the logo?"

Mr Pringle made out the name.

"They're tradespeople. Something to do with stationery supplies?"

Shirley's voice was tight. "That could be them. They pretended to Sammy they wanted to store paper. Those cartons are all labelled A4 and stuff, in different colours."

"How intelligent," Mr Pringle observed mildly, "because the weight would correspond, if you take my meaning. Nothing to arouse undue suspicion. I remember a most interesting fraud investigation in Nottingham – "

"Hey!" Irwin's thought processes were slower but he'd got

there. "You mean, the rest of the gang could be in that truck?"

"More than likely, I fear," Mr Pringle replied. "I didn't spot Dulce but he could have been hidden inside. Under the circumstances, if we could make a little more speed . . . "

Irwin did a racing change, found a cog and put his foot down hard.

Big Joe squealed from the back, "She ain't used to this kinda treatment!"

The lorry flung its occupants from left to right and back again. In the back, Sammy whooped with terror and delight as the redheaded whore charged down the highway, swaying dementedly.

Chapter Eleven

Later on the 18th

Louis had been half-way down the rocks when he heard the stationery truck. The vehicle had turned in off the highway and was headed towards the ranch. He scrambled back up, his ankle so stiff he could hardly bear it. Dehydration had brought delusions, he kept reaching for hand-holds that weren't there. In the distance there was this wonderful shimmering blue lake. If only he could reach that water!

Somehow he found a niche big enough to squeeze into. His hands shook, his whole body wanted to give up but fear kept him where he was.

He'd heard the excitement earlier; sound carried in this clear air. He'd heard the seedy looking guy in the stetson say both men in the barn were dead. Louis still found that difficult to believe! He hadn't heard any shots so what the hell had happened? Then Pringle and Mavis Bignell had arrived and taken a look – and come out looking pig sick. Louis could've screamed when he saw Pringle wheeling out the cash: how dare he steal it!

Was one of the dead men John? It couldn't have been a police helicopter after all. Was the other Gino? And if Gino had killed John, what had happened to *him*?

Had the sun affected his mind, was that it? Maybe Louis had dreamed the whole thing? Maybe he never even saw that canvas-sided truck with the picture of Mavis Bignell drive away with all the money.

Would to Christ he had never met Mavis Bignell!

Salt filled the cracks in his skin. A fierce, dry wind had added to the torment. There wasn't enough shade. He would die of thirst long before any rescue came. Was that the police arriving down there now?

The stationery truck halted by the ranch house. A man Louis didn't recognise jumped out, handgun at the ready, and disappeared inside. After a moment or two, he re-emerged and the truck continued up towards the barn. This time, three men got out. One of them was – *Gino*! His hands were tied in front and the other two strangers had their guns trained on him.

Instinct kept Louis silent. He watched the body language without hearing all they were saying. The man with the gun was gesticulating, obviously telling Gino to enter the barn. Behind, the second stranger waited by the truck. He carried an automatic rifle.

Gino looked different, his hair was all frizzed up. And if he was alive, who the hell was in the barn? Louis watched as his friend frowned at the sight of Irwin's belongings, and kicked a pan lid. It rolled a few feet.

"Don't know what's been going on but this is the place."

"Open it up, Gino. Show us the money."

"OK, OK . . . "

From his perch, Louis knew he should yell before it was too late. That old truck couldn't have gotten far, they could catch up with it, provided he and Gino could deal with these two first. Which, given the circumstances, was nothing but a sick joke.

Gino lifted bound hands and tugged at the door. He eased it open a crack and went inside. Louis and the other two waited. He came out again slowly, very pale.

"Someone's been here, Al," he said. "They've killed Ozal and John and they've taken the money."

"What?"

Up on his ledge, Louis's brain reeled. Who had gotten inside and murdered . . . hadn't he been watching like a cat at a mouse hole the whole damn time?

He watched dumbly as the man with the handgun rushed forward and Gino's leg shot out; it was the only chance he had. Even in his shocked state, Louis could see what Gino intended to do – to grab the gun as the man's body fell past – but it didn't work out because the other stranger whipped up his rifle. At a range of less than twenty feet even Louis Carlson couldn't have missed.

The body jerked and twitched as it tumbled into the dirt. No one would lie like that if they could help it, it was too uncomfortable. Blood spilled. Gino's blood. The human being Louis had depended on – had even considered double-crossing such a short time ago – was dying down there. Louis had lived all his life in make-believe land: in the dust was reality, and he had done nothing to prevent it happening.

So now all three were dead, just as he'd planned in New York. He'd never felt so miserable in his life. Even the realisation that Beth and the boys were safe now that Ozal was gone, did little to help. He was alone! How was he going to manage?

In Homicide, spirits had lifted. There was nothing like having something to go on, everyone agreed. Having a result was even better. Most cheerful of all was the captain. He'd summoned Hocht and Purcelle to his office.

"How d'you like that? Son-of-a-bitch!"

"Huh?"

"Relax, take a seat. Have a cigar. Name Del Freeman mean anything?"

"Nope."

"Well, it damn well should!" The captain was so jovial it was painful. "Because it was your idea to have those passes re-checked . . . and guess which name didn't check out, lieutenant?"

"Del Freeman?" Hocht repeated woodenly.

"Right! Ask me where that pass finally turned up?"

"Where did the aforesaid pass turn up, sir?"

"In a police uniform, in the trunk of a certain patrol car. One that definitely shouldn't have been in the compound, that showed signs of wear and tear compatible with forcing open an automatic gate." Eyes were much more interested now.

"The one that we presume – "

"The hell with presumption. The one we *know* must've been used for the heist."

"Anything else we've found out about Del Freeman and his pass?"

"It's only a preliminary report . . . seems like he had a ladyfriend. Used to visit her, wearing his uniform."

"Oh?" Hocht's gaze narrowed.

"She used cheap lipstick. You know, the sort that smudges?"

"I know."

Purcelle said quietly, "The same sort Mrs Beeker used?"

"Got the report?"

Purcelle handed over the file he'd been carrying. The captain spread it open on the desk alongside his own notes. He checked the file first. "According to this, when she was strangled Mrs Beeker was wearing a lip rouge called 'Desert Hibiscus'. Desert Hibiscus? What kinda hibiscus grows in a desert?"

"And on Del Freeman's uniform?" Hocht was too strung up to play along.

"According to this, nothing definite, except . . . " The captain *wanted* him to play. "We got a preliminary breakdown of lanolin content, etc etc. And we got a preliminary on the possible brands, one of which includes a list of names, of which one of them is . . . ?"

"Evening Primrose?" asked Hocht politely.

The phone rang. The captain answered it tersely, "Yeah . . . " They watched his ballpoint move across the paper. "Yeah . . . identified as who?" It was impossible to read the name upside down. "Thanks." He hung up. "That was the morgue. One of the bodies from the Beaux Rêves was carrying a gun. Recently fired."

"At the guards?"

"No. The owner was found under the rubble in the ballroom." He grimaced, "What the hell . . . recently fired at who? Is there something I don't know about? Was anyone else shot in there last night? Are you keeping something from me, Hocht?"

"Not as far as I am aware, sir."

"Go to hell! And Hocht."

"Sir?"

"Next time, say thank you."

"Thank you, sir."

It couldn't last but as Mavis said, it had been a most exhilarating experience and at least no one had been killed. Even Shirley hadn't come off too badly.

"That's because I landed on top of you."

"Thank God you're not heavy, that's all I can say. How's your arm?"

Shirley raised it carefully.

"Not too bad . . . I think."

"I dunno," Mavis said crossly. "What a country. First we get tied up, then the money gets stolen, someone tries to blow up Frank Sinatra, that man gets his throat cut, now this . . . "

They were sitting in the wreckage as Irwin and Big Joe mourned the departure of the inside front wheel, the sheared axle, plus the fact the lorry was now on its side. The red-headed whore had, in every sense of the word, bitten the dust. Fortunately, it had all happened in slow motion. Shaken but not badly damaged, they crawled out and tested their joints for breakages.

Mr Pringle, in his uncomfortable jeans, stood bow-legged, scanning the horizon behind them.

"I fear the rest of the gang cannot be long in coming . . . once they have discovered the bodies, that the money has vanished . . . retribution, etc etc." He pulled himself together. As leader of the party, it behoved him to maintain morale. Nevertheless it was difficult. Such wide open spaces, such a lack of telephone kiosks.

Sammy dragged the last carton clear of the wreckage. "Guess I better ask Charlene if we can have a loan of her papa's car."

"I beg your pardon?" Was there life in these parts?

"What a good idea," Shirley recognised the wire fencing. "I'd forgotten there was a short cut from here to the back of their property. Off you go then, Sammy. Don't stop to talk to Charlene. Those bad men could be here any minute."

"Yes, Grandma."

"You'd better ask Mr Brand to call the police . . . " She looked apologetically at Mr Pringle, who didn't protest. The need for assistance was now urgent. "Tell them," Shirley instructed, "we've had an accident and some bad men with guns are headed this way. That's all."

"Yes, Grandma!" Sammy ran down the bank and leaped over the fence.

"Better to keep it simple," she said apologetically, "then there's a chance he might get it right."

"Yes," Mr Pringle replied. Was there still time to effect a disappearance before either the gang or authority intervened? Sammy was loping away into the distance.

"How long will it take him?"

"It's over a quarter of a mile to the house. I don't know whether he'll find anyone at home. The hands could be anywhere, at the far end of the property, for instance."

In other words, he'd better think quickly.

"Irwin, Joseph . . . Might I have a word." They listened to his proposals.

Gino hadn't taken long to die. When it was over, the one called Al watched as the other man kicked the corpse viciously. "I told you, no double-cross, Kuminsky! Stupid bastard."

"Come on, let's see inside." The two walked into the barn. When they re-emerged, Al was much more thoughtful. He crouched to examine Irwin's possessions.

"He was telling the truth about that. Looks like whoever it was killed those two, emptied this stuff out. These tyre marks are fresh."

"He was making room for the money?"

"Can't be any other reason I can think of. Who'd have things like this?"

"Anyone living out of a truck . . . like . . . " They stared at one another.

"Like that crazy-looking outfit we passed awhile back?"

"Why not? Can't have been time for anyone else."

They dragged Gino's body into the barn. Five minutes later, the dust was settling in the wake of their passage.

Even in his desperate state, Louis knew he had a choice. Down there was Pringle's battered limousine. A long way behind the rocks was his own hire car. He was tempted, especially at the thought of water available in the house, but he had the sense to head for the hire car. The police could arrive any minute. Suppose they found him surrounded by three corpses and a helicopter? How could anyone squeeze out of that situation?

God, his ankle hurt like crazy. It was swollen beneath his trouser leg, it was so bad. Crawling was the only way. It could take for ever!

Mr Pringle inspected Big Joe's tool kit.

"I fear the possibilities are limited."

"Sorry 'bout that, hadn't anticipated this kinda operation." The elfin locks were dejected.

"Don't worry, we may yet succeed." Mr Pringle realised he

must keep up a cheery front. "Irwin, may I enquire if this vehicle is insured?" The face of the prophet was expressive. "I imagine you would also be reluctant to pay for it to be towed away?"

"You bet I would!"

"Can't do anything with it no more, though," Joe opined. "The old bitch is dead."

"She contains items we can use, however. Plus your wire-cutters, that wrench and a hammer."

Once his troops understood the destructive nature of the enterprise, they joined in willingly. As chief tactician, Mr Pringle strove to reassure them.

"The idea . . . is based on a certain chapter . . . in Gibbon's, *Decline and Fall* . . . " He and Big Joe were struggling to cut lengths of barbed wire from the paddock boundary fencing.

"Gibbon a military man?"

Mr Pringle's knowledge was limited.

"I'm not entirely sure," he confessed. He didn't know how that particular chapter had ended either, the book had been due back at the library. "However, I think we can rely on Gibbon. His reputation is sound . . . Right, we string these across the road and tension them using the posts. A bit tighter at your end? The original idea, using ropes slung from trees, was to unhorse the cavalry. Being Roman, they didn't have stirrups – and we are talking of a different form of horse-power – but the principle is the same." He remembered another chapter.

"What a pity we cannot devise pilii. They were most effective when embedded in the enemy's shields."

"Always been a pacifist myself, 'cept like today, when men come after me with guns."

"My sentiments exactly, Joseph. However, perhaps we ought to press on. Irwin, if you've finished . . . ?" The prophet scrambled up from where he'd been hiding cartons in the ditch.

"Safe enough for the time being."

"Splendid. Now, your strength, combined with that sledge hammer . . . "

Mrs Bignell, handkerchief round her face, was sprinkling a mixture of oil and diesel over the white canvas. She watched the destruction of the gear box and engine mounting. A sludge-like substance oozed across the road in an ever-widening, turgid ripple.

"Yuk!" Big Joe shook his head over it.

"The old girl sure was co-operative with all that gunge in her belly."

"I carried a spare can," Irwin said sulkily, "just never got round to doing the change, that's all."

"Additional oil, did you say?" Mr Pringle beamed, "I think we can make use of that."

Mavis watched him search the wreckage. "He's forgotten how poorly he was feeling before." Shirley gazed at the treacherous patch of diesel.

"Hate to think what the traffic cops could charge us with if they came along."

"Oh, dear! Does this road get busy on a Sunday?"

Shirley laughed weakly. "Just be our bad luck, wouldn't it?"

Mrs Bignell looked severely at the heavens, "Considering it *is* Sunday, it's time we had a bit of help, never mind bad luck."

The fan was sending a jet of cold air over Louis Carlson's foot. Numbness lessened the pain, he could think straight at last. He must concentrate on what to do next. For a start, he was damned if he'd let Gino's murderers get hold of the money! As for Pringle, Bignell and those two freaks . . .

Louis inhaled the cold air. Thank God it was his left foot, he could hit the gas with his right and he needed to, to catch up. He couldn't remember a scenario that fitted but twenty-three million was reason enough to go for it. Beth and the kids were safe which gave him a warm feeling inside. The money would buy them the best possible future. Courage began to return; he'd think of something

Shirley heard a familiar sound and shaded her eyes. "It's the Brands' cattle wagon, I think. Yes, here it comes! Good for Sammy. Damn, what's that?"

They turned simultaneously. The other vehicle was approaching fast, from the direction of the ranch. It shimmered in the heat but its silhouette was unmistakable. Mr Pringle suddenly felt breathless.

"Action stations!" he ordered hoarsely. "Ignite your rags. Keep your heads down."

"Be careful, dear!" They were scuttling in all directions like crabs.

"Wait until I give the word."

"Sure."

"Joseph, make sure the foam rubber is smouldering. Mavis, Shirley – get out of sight."

"We are!"

"Lower your bottom, Mavis!" It was his particular joy, he wasn't having it endangered.

Automatic gunfire spattered. The van was within yards of the wrecked lorry which had been pushed into the middle of the road.

"Now!" yelled G D H Pringle. He and Irwin tightened the barbed wire, lifting the strands deliberately high.

Behind the wheel, Al reacted, slamming on the brakes as the van hit first the wire, then the lethal stretch of tarmac. As the skid began, the rear offside tyre deflated.

The steering wheel spun between Al's hands as the skid went out of control. At the side of the road, Mr Pringle issued a stream of commands.

Big Joe flung his burning rags on to the sludge. Mavis threw hers on to the white canvas. Smoke rose thickly and from either side, Big Joe and Irwin added to it with smouldering chunks of foam which filled the air with acrid toxic fumes.

Approaching the scene, the laden cattle wagon began to lose speed.

"My, oh, my! They gone crazy, Sammy? That's a real mess they made."

"Yes, Mr Brand."

The stationery van appeared through the smoke, heading sideways towards them, all four wheels fully locked.

"Hell's teeth!"

Sammy clung to his seat. Mr Brand was a little slow in finding reverse.

"Shit!"

"Yesmrbrand!"

But the van slammed into a piece of wreckage. It juddered, slewed round before continuing, at right angles, off the road and into the ditch.

Amazement made Mr Pringle gasp: it had been a success!

Sammy was already out of the wagon and peering through the windscreen.

"There's two of them, Mr Brand. One's armed." The cattle owner jumped from the cab, shotgun at the ready.

"Hand that over to the boy . . . nice and slow or I'll blow your head off. Got it, Sammy?"

"Yes, Mr Brand."

"Put it in my cab. Any more guns in there?"

Mr Pringle heard the reply.

"Here's Al's . . . " The handgun clattered on to the highway, "Guess he won't be needing it no more."

Joy disappeared in an instant. Oh God, he thought, all this carnage and now I've killed a man: I'm no better than they are.

The cattle owner touched his hat as Shirley and Mavis clambered up to the road. "Mornin' Miz Callaghan. How're y' doing?"

"Nicely thank you, Jesse. We've been having a spot of bother."

"So Sammy said. We called the police. They should be here, soon."

"Ah . . . " Mr Pringle's frozen wits began to work. He introduced himself and explained. Mr Brand stared at the pile of cartons.

"The missing cash is in them boxes?"

"We haven't bothered to count it."

"Me and the wife watched Frank Sinatra on the TV."

"It was – is – our intention to hand it over intact to the proper authorities, in order that Mrs Callaghan may claim the reward."

"Uh-huh."

"If we wait for the police to arrive, they may take the credit themselves, and we lack transport."

Mr Brand was quick off the mark.

"C'm on, get movin'! Get these boxes on board! Move the cattle up front, Sammy. Shove everything in behind. Fast as you can, boys."

As they toiled, Irwin muttered, "He's bound to want a share. Anyone else comes along, won't be nothing left for you and me, Big Joe."

Mr Brand brandished his weapon.

"Hurry, hurry! Sammy, you come here an' take a hold of my ol' gun. Keep it pointed at that there truck. If either one of those bad men so much as sticks a big toe out before the police git here, you can blow his foot off. Think you can manage that?"

"Yes, Mr Brand!"

"That all right by you, Miz Callaghan?"

"You don't take your eyes off those two, not even if Charlene turns up. Promise me now," Shirley said sternly.

"I promise."

"And don't say a word to the police. We'll be back quick as we can, understand?"

"Yes, Grandma."

The wagon lumbered peacefully towards Boulder. A beast in the pen behind blew soft moist breath over the back of Mrs Bignell's neck. She said pleasantly, "I must say you get a good view of the road, sitting this high."

"'Specially of the cops," Mr Brand growled. "Here they come . . ."

Patrol cars hurtled past, sirens wailing.

"We got all that money in the back and they never even suspected."

"I hope they don't either," Shirley said fervently. "Mavis, did you manage to see the men in the van?"

"I did. Neither of them was Enrico Dulce," Mr Pringle replied quietly.

"You two better watch out then. You're not out of the woods yet."

Mavis had another worry. "Goodness! I hope those police cars slow down before they reach that diesel."

Necks twisted round but not that of Mr Pringle. "I don't think I can bear to look."

"We're too far away," Mr Brand comforted. "See, there's Boulder City ahead."

There were flashing lights and the traffic cop was signalling him to stop. Because he was tired, Louis Carlson was on the scene before he could avoid it. Then he scolded himself. Why should he be suspected? All he had to do was keep his nerve. He wound down his window. "What's going on?"

"There's been an accident, you'll need to make a diversion." Louis glimpsed limp shreds of painted white canvas amid the smoking heap. His heart began to pound.

"What happened to that?"

"We're hoping the passenger in the other truck will tell us. He's in shock, the driver's dead."

Louis spotted Sammy sitting in the back of a police car.

"That the passenger?" he asked, apparently carelessly. The traffic cop scowled.

"Nah, he's a dumbo. He was pointing a shotgun at the two of 'em like it was a hold-up."

There was shouting from the breakdown team. Those spraying chemicals on to the diesel stopped to give a hand. The stationery truck was hauled back on to the road. As the door swung open, Louis could see it was empty inside.

He thanked the cop and drove off. This needed thinking out. Even if Pringle plus the cash had managed to vanish, Louis Carlson was willing to bet Boulder City was still the intended destination. What he had to do was get there fast.

Sammy enjoyed being the centre of attention. The cops were interested in the dead man so he boasted where they might find two more bodies, one of them Mr Freeman's. Then he remembered what he'd promised Grandma. She'd be real mad if he told them she'd taken the money to Boulder City; he'd better keep quiet till she got back.

Patrol cars, helicopters, ambulances, all the apparatus of law enforcement began to focus on the ranch. Communications were established. News began to filter through to headquarters. Relevant items reached Hocht and Purcelle.

"When our boys got to the barn, they found there were three bodies, not two. The third had been gunned down. The dumbo takes a look and says this was Mr Kuminsky but he hadn't been there before. Then the passenger in the stationery truck decides to talk. Says *they* were there earlier, there was a row and his boss shot the guy – refuses to say *why*, we're working on that – but claims he once heard his boss refer to Kuminsky as Gino."

"So?" said Hocht.

"There's a Gino Millar on file, fits the description of Kuminsky. They're working on it. Then when they look at the other two bodies, the dumbo identifies one of them as Mr Freeman." Gary Hocht stared. Purcelle nodded.

"Yep. They're faxing the photos through."

★

At the Greyhound stop in front of the casino at Boulder City, Mavis asked wearily, "What's the number of our bus?"

"It'll have Flagstaff on the front, I hope."

"It's going to be another long day," she sighed.

"We'll break the journey at Flagstaff but we'll stay at a different motel." She smiled, gratefully.

"We're on our way home, that's the main thing. I'm glad you suggested Mr Brand take charge. He'll make sure Shirley gets the reward."

"I sincerely hope so."

"Irwin was just being greedy. He shouldn't have been. That lorry wasn't insured and you gave him enough of the float to put a deposit on a new one."

"Yes." It troubled Mr Pringle's conscience far less than he'd anticipated. Without that lorry, he and Mavis might not have escaped, it was sufficient justification. When Mavis had suggested any remaining float be put towards the over-sixties' Christmas outing, he'd agreed with that, too. To whom should he send the receipts, he wondered? Enrico Dulce, care of the Nevada police department, perhaps?

"Shirley will explain. I don't think we need worry about the police or Mrs Shuckenhauser and her friends. I hope we see her again." He stared in disbelief. "Shirley, silly!"

"Ah, yes . . . I think this bus may be ours. You find a seat. I'll make sure our luggage is on board."

A car cruising past as if in search of a parking space, pulled up smartly beyond the stop. Louis Carlson ground his teeth as he saw the care with which Pringle stowed the two suitcases. God knows what had happened to the rest of the cash but Louis Carlson was entitled to what was in those bags. He'd earned it! Those damn limeys weren't having a cent!

"What a good thing our Ameripasses hadn't run out," Mavis said as he joined her. "From Denver, have you worked what day of the week it'll be when we get back to London?"

"May I have your attention, ladies and gen'lemen." The coach driver was dark-haired and buxom. Her mushroom-grey pants fitted so sleekly, Mr Pringle stopped listening. Mavis nudged him; the announcement sounded important.

". . . those of our employees who have been dismissed

because of their unlawful strike action have threatened reprisals. We, on the management, can assure you however, that your safety is our first concern."

From the back of the coach a passenger shouted, "What have they said they'll do?"

The driver was dismissive. "Oh, you know . . . attacking the coaches, stuff like that. Nobody is taking that kind of talk *seriously*."

"Why not? Suppose they do?" Anxiety spread among the elderly. The driver attempted to quell it.

"As I told you before, ladies and gen'lemen, your safety is our first concern. Now, if you'll excuse me, I'd like to get this show on the road."

She engaged gears dexterously. Mavis was anxious.

"Does she mean like highwaymen?"

"I've no idea," Mr Pringle said tiredly. "Let's wait and see, shall we?"

They turned on to route 93, heading for Kingman. As his body tried to find a comfortable position, he remembered why it was he'd promised himself he would never travel by coach again.

Purcelle crashed through the door of the office this time. "Hey, listen. This Gino Millar had a nephew, John Millar . . . they released his army record a short time ago."

"Not nice?"

"Not nice."

"So?"

"Look at these. The one the dumbo identified as Freeman, here's that picture . . . and this John Millar in his army days . . . and this is a copy of the security pass which was in the uniform with the lipstick on it." The three were of the same man. Hocht sighed.

"So, Judy Beeker's killer." He compared two of them; one, enlarged from an army group, fresh-faced and crop-headed, apparently full of promise. The last with the tongue hanging out of the wide dead mouth. "Strangled?"

"Uh-huh."

"An eye for an eye . . . " He examined another photograph. "Jesus, is this the best they could manage of *him*?"

"There were others but he looked even more grotesque."

"Is the autopsy report available?"

"Not yet. According to the preliminary examination." Purcelle read from it: "'As the second subject tripped, he apparently reached out with both hands to break his fall but didn't see the rotor, due to visual handicap' – for Chrissake, why not say he was blind? – 'Subject's throat was extended, he hit the edge of the blade at speed, with two hundred and five pounds of body weight behind the impact. That section of blade is manufactured of stainless steel although not particularly sharp. The artery was only partially severed. Second subject did not die immediately. From gouge marks in the dirt, it appears he continued with attempts to escape but his foot remained trapped in the handle of the fuel container. Report concludes: second subject bled for upwards of fifteen minutes before succumbing.'"

"Second subject having just strangled first subject?"

"Evidence would appear to indicate it, yes."

With the black and white photograph in his hands, Hocht tried to imagine how he'd feel after cherishing a memory for thirty years.

"She's agreed . . . ?"

"Yep."

"She's been warned?" Again Purcelle nodded.

It was the same interview room. They treated Monica with grave courtesy. "Coffee, Miss Moffat?"

"No, thank you." It was pushed across the shining hygenic surface.

"Do you recognise this man, Miss Moffat?" Monica gripped her hands tightly.

"Yes."

"And was he the man you saw in the patrol car last night?" Another nod. "Would you please tell us his name?"

"John Ozal Halling."

"Thank you, Miss Moffat."

It was the commotion made by other passengers which woke Mr Pringle. Then he spotted the cause. Keeping pace with the coach, in the outside lane, was a car; in the driver's seat was Louis Carlson.

"Mavis, look!"

Other passengers were shouting now.

"Will you look at that!"

"Why doesn't he overtake?"

"Tell our driver," Mavis was thoroughly frightened. "Warn her who he is."

There was excitement throughout the coach.

"It's one of those goddamn strikers!"

"If he's overtaking, why doesn't he get in front?"

"What an idiot!"

"Could be an accident – "

"Hey, miss. Look in your mirror."

"I've seen him." She increased the speed; so did Louis Carlson. "Don't be concerned, ladies and gen'lemen. Your safety is of the highest priority." She began speaking into her cell phone.

Coach and car were neck and neck as passengers clung to their seats with arthritic hands.

The police officer was actually enjoying this Press conference.

"So the Brits had nothing to do with the heist?"

"If you recall, it was one of the actors who made the accusation. He now admits it was without foundation. We believe them to be innocent."

"Including the Pringle guy?"

"Including G D Pringle, yes."

"You say the money was handed in to a bank packed in stationery cartons?"

"A suspect has confirmed this was the plan for concealing the money for onward transportation, which we intercepted, of course."

"D'you expect the final amount to tally?"

"We hope so. The bank are checking it out."

"Does this wrap it up?"

"Basically, yes. Mrs Callaghan has been able to clear up various points – "

"Captain, when can we talk to Mrs Callaghan?"

Louis Carlson was suffering from exposure and lack of sleep, otherwise he might have noticed the fuel warning light, bright as a malevolent red eye.

He wasn't a clever man, the only plan he could devise was to force the bus off the highway at the next junction and use his car to block the road. He would then demand those two bags. He didn't intend to hurt anyone, not even Pringle . . . the engine faltered.

Louis looked at the gauge; the warning light didn't even flicker. Aw, shit! The engine coughed, surged and faltered again. He was travelling too fast. He lifted his foot. The coach driver slowed as well, she wasn't going to let him tuck in behind. He hadn't enough power to get ahead. Bitch! Bitch! Bitch! Louis pounded the horn.

An articulated truck heading in the opposite direction came out of a curve and saw the car limping towards him in the centre of the road. Louis had time to scream "Beth!" but that was all.

"I think it might be wise, when it's our turn, if we refer to ourselves as Mr and Mrs Thompson."

"Yes, dear." The police were taking statements from every passenger on the bus. They had reached the couple two rows ahead. "Will you do the talking?"

"If you wish."

"Enrico must've been very determined, poor soul. D'you think he intended to kill us?"

"Ssh!"

"What happened? Did that articulated lorry knock him off the road, or what?" Mr Pringle was in the window seat; he had no intention of describing the dreadful sight. As they'd jacked up the six wheeler, the hire car was nothing but a compressed metal coffin beneath.

"It might be better if I kept that for the police," he murmured gently.

"Will you tell them who he was?" whispered Mavis.

"Mr and Mrs Thompson wouldn't have known."

"Oh, no. I forgot. Of course they wouldn't."

They caught the plane at Denver and changed at St Louis, dusty, weary, too tired to notice the newspapers which featured their photographs. By the time they reached New York they were yesterday's news. They passed through immigration and customs controls and became part of one of the amorphous crowds, five hundred strong, shuffling along a departure channel.

Mavis wriggled in her uncomfortable economy seat. "I hope I

was wrong about the gas."

"So do I!"

"Pardon me . . . " It was a keen-eyed American matron, "Haven't I seen you on the TV?"

Mr Pringle was immediately deaf but Mavis ventured a cautious, "Quite possibly."

"I knew I was right! Would you please sign my little girl's autograph book."

With pen poised, Mavis murmured, "You do understand . . . my husband and I are travelling incognito. For security reasons."

"Oh, sure! I won't breathe a word!" Mr Pringle's eyes were closed. He heard the scrawl and raised a lid. In a bold swirl, Mrs Bignell had inscribed, M H T.

Beneath was a crown surmounting a crooked Big Ben. The matron was enchanted.

"I'm so sorry you had to give up ruling England."

Mavis was extremely gracious.

"We were disappointed, too. But one has ensured one's place in history, one did save England, for a time."

As the matron backed away, Mr Pringle heard, "She's so much nicer than her photographs, so charming. I never realised her hair was auburn, I thought she was a blonde."

He looked at Mavis sternly, "Impersonation is a punishable offence."

"Oh, pooh!" said Mrs Bignell.

Chapter Twelve

8.00 p.m. on the 29th

There was mellow contentment in the bar of the Bricklayers; Mavis, hair coiffed, magnificent bosom resplendent in fuchsia silk, had made her reappearance to appreciative growls. Once these had been acknowledged she managed to notice Mrs Ellis on her stool.

"Edith!"

"Mavis!" They embraced.

"You're back."

"So are you."

They considered one another again.

"Did you have a lovely holiday?"

"Oh, yes!" Mrs Ellis glistened after her third glass of port. "Wasn't Frank Sinatra wonderful?"

"I'm sure he was, dear, but we never got to Las Vegas."

"What!" Edith Ellis could scarcely credit it.

Mrs Bignell glanced at Mr Pringle, slumbering in his usual chair, the pub cat on his knee. "Sad, wasn't it. By all accounts, it must've been very exciting?"

Mrs Ellis clutched at her chest, "I shall never forget it. In the dark, when that bomb went off, I thought my last moment had come. You must've seen it on the television?"

Mavis sighed.

"Not even that, I'm afraid. We were tucked up in bed in Boulder City when it happened."

"What a shame! What sort of holiday was yours then?"

Mrs Bignell hesitated. "Fairly quiet. We saw quite a bit of the countryside, in between the filming." One of the regulars handed her his empty glass.

"So what did you think of America, Mavie?" Mrs Bignell

concentrated on drawing the beer before pronouncing her verdict.

"It's big . . . very big in parts. Lovely weather. We didn't have a drop of rain. But I wouldn't want to go back until they've got rid of all those guns."

"Guns?" Mrs Ellis was astonished. "I never saw any. Except the ones the police have on their hips. And the security men, while they were protecting the money." The customer snorted.

"They weren't much use, seeing that gang pinched the lot."

"Yes, but the police got it all back. Without firing a single shot," Mrs Ellis added pointedly. "'Ere, Mavis, I've just remembered. The day after it happened there was a photo of a man with a gun on the telly – "

"Perhaps that's what I was thinking of," Mrs Bignell interrupted smoothly, "that'll be one pound thirty, ta."

"No, listen." Mrs Ellis had become excited, "They kept saying this man was a Mr G D Pringle! You should've heard the names they were calling him."

In the Bricklayers indignation was mixed with incredulity.

"That's what I said," she agreed loudly, "I said to my daughter-in-law, if somebody is trying to suggest our Mr P would sit there waving a pistol, like some totally irresponsible person, that somebody doesn't know what he's talking about."

As if in acknowledgement, the unconscious figure in the corner gave a small inoffensive snore.

"As if he would, bless him."

"Must have been somebody like him, I suppose," Mavis said daringly.

"No, it wasn't *like* him at all. Not if you actually *knew* him, that is."

One good turn deserved another: God had heard her prayers about the gas. "Talking about photographs," Mavis smiled benignly. "What about that clever grandson of yours? Did you take any of him while you were over there?"

As if by magic, a bulging folder appeared in Mrs Ellis's hand.

"They're a little bit out of focus because I forgot to pack my spectacles," she admitted, "but I can tell you who they all are."